RENEGADE RAMPAGE

ROCKY MOUNTAIN SAINT BOOK 9

B.N. RUNDELL

WOLFPACK
PUBLISHING
— EST 2013 —

Renegade Rampage
(Rocky Mountain Saint Book 9)
B.N. Rundell

Paperback Edition
© Copyright 2019 B.N. Rundell

Wolfpack Publishing
6032 Wheat Penny Avenue
Las Vegas, NV 89122

wolfpackpublishing.com

Paperback ISBN 978-1-64119-576-8
eBook ISBN 978-1-64119-575-1

Library of Congress Control Number: 2019930297

Patience. *Some say patience is a virtue. Some say patience is the excuse used by lazy people for a lack of action. Others will admit that patience has nothing to do with biding one's time while waiting, but rather the determined perseverance through trials and obstacles to achieve a goal. Whatever it is and whatever definition you prefer, my loving wife was given an abundance of it. She has certainly needed it as my "first-line editor." Every word I've written is heard and/or read by my wife before anyone. She has waded hand in hand with me through the muck and mire that I call writing to help me out the other side with some semblance of a story. And since she is the only person that I'm related to that has ever been introduced to the many characters of my books, I am blessed by her. Her patience with me is amazing, a lesser woman could not have put up with me. I am thankful every day for her and for her being my life-partner and so I dedicate this book to my beloved. Thank you, sweetheart!*

RENEGADE RAMPAGE

LOBO, THE BIG GREY WOLF, HAD BEEN A CONSTANT COMPANION of Tate Saint since the man found him in the northernmost mountains of the Absaroka Range. This man, who had become known as the Rocky Mountain Saint, had been traveling with a new friend and companion named Knuckles, who he met on the riverboat on his return from St. Louis. It was when the crusty old mountain man joined up with what he thought was a greenhorn. His task was to show Tate the mountains and Indians of the north country. That was when they witnessed an attack by a wolf pack on some mustangs and ultimately Tate found the pup that would become his friend. But now Lobo had a companion of his own, a black wolf pup with orange eyes that pierced the wilderness, and although still a pup, he was showing he would soon be as big as his father. Tate was certain the pup was an offspring of one of Lobo's midnight rendezvous that he was known to take in answer to long lonesome howls that filled the black of night. Those howls that also sprang forth from the beast and friend periodically.

"What are you so thoughtful about," asked Maggie, Tate's

redheaded wife of over a dozen years. Their family of four was traveling together through the Wind River mountains, enroute to visit the land of wonders and waters that Tate had told them about many times. The two rode side by side, their two children following behind the packhorses. And Maggie's Irish curiosity showed in the twinkling eyes of the freckle-faced imp Tate lovingly called his wife of marvels.

Tate looked to Maggie and answered, "Oh, just rememberin' when Lobo brought that pup back home. Never thought I'd see the day when he would even tolerate a pup, much less bring one home. Makes me wonder what happened to the one that whelped him."

Maggie laughed with her lilting mirth that always brought a smile to Tate, "Well, one thing I be mighty certain of, and that is that pup is like his daddy in ever' way but color. And those eyes! It's like he's starin' out of the darkness and right through you!"

Tate chuckled at his wife's description, but he had also wondered about the eyes that appeared to be black one moment and glowing orange the next. But the pup had shown a special liking to Sadie, his daughter of just past seven years old, almost a mirror image of her mother, and still full of all the mischief imaginable for one so pretty and petite. While Lobo had always been the companion of Tate and often with Sean, his son of twelve years and a little more, the black wolf, now called Indigo, had chosen to spend his time with Maggie and Sadie. While Lobo was beginning to show his age, the youthful playfulness of Indigo often wore him out, forcing the pup to seek a playful companion elsewhere. Sadie was always happy to oblige and showed her willingness by burying her face in his thick fur, yet the wolf had always been protective and gentle with the girl.

Maggie looked to her man, who stood just over six feet tall with broad shoulders and narrow hips, and noticed he had again grown pensive, and she wanted to ask, but didn't want to spoil his reverie. They had been together since they first met when she came west searching for her missing father and Tate guided her through the mountains and helped her locate the last of her family. They had enjoyed many an adventure and wonderful times together, and she knew her man, probably as well as he knew himself. He had often shared the story of his early life; how he came from Missouri when he was still a teen and alone, to explore the Rocky Mountains. That exploration had long been a dream he shared with his schoolteacher father, and when his father was killed, he set out alone to fulfill that dream and became a man of the mountains. She knew he had been in the mountains many years before they met, he even had an Indian wife before her, but he had always been a part of these mountains since and had grown in the knowledge of the ways of the wilderness. He had shared with her that the trail they now traveled had often been used by the Arapaho as they journeyed from their summer camp higher in the Wind River range to the winter camp in the lower foothills.

She looked at him again and saw he was more attentive to the trail and asked, "Were you remembering?"

Tate looked to her and let a grin paint his face, "How do you do that? Just cuz I wasn't talkin' an' you look at me an' know what I'm thinkin' as certain as if I was talkin' out loud!"

Maggie chuckled, "I just know you. When you grow quiet, you're either working out a problem, planning something, or remembering."

"I was remembering the first time I came through here. I left Knuckles, that old-timer mountain man I told you 'bout, with the Shoshoni and his wife, Pinequanáh, Smells of Sugar, and their son, Chochoco, and then had a time with them missionaries."

"You still think Knuckles will be with the Shoshoni?"

"I'm hopin' so, but ya' never know 'bout this country. Where we're headed is an area where you're liable to find Blackfeet, Nez Perce, Gros Ventre, Shoshoni and Crow. All of 'em like to come to the land of many waters. And don't none of 'em get along too well. Of 'em all, the one bunch that don't seem to get along too well with others is the Blackfeet. When some of the tribes signed that treaty in '51, ain't none of 'em been too happy with the lands they were assigned. An' the Blackfeet, they didn't even sign! Course, the Gros Ventre used to be allied with the Blackfeet or part o' their bands, but not'ny more.

"But, the Shoshoni have been sorta peaceful with the whites an' the area we're goin' to is mostly their territory, so, we'll be alright. But I don't know if Knuckles'll still be there." He glanced over at his wife, watching her rock to the gait of her buckskin, showing herself comfortable in the saddle. He always admired his wife's ability to adapt to the lifestyle of the mountains that was so different from the life she knew in her younger years in the cities. She had become adept with a bow, a rifle, and her pocket Dragoon, and learned from the many Indian women about the plants and herbs of the mountains. She was a wonder to him and he was proud of her and never failed to show that pride and love.

"How long were the two of you together?" asked Maggie. Tate seldom shared details of his life before Maggie, unless prodded by her curiosity. It wasn't that he was prone to keep secrets, he just didn't like talking about himself.

"Oh, wasn't that long, couple months maybe, but he taught me a lot about the Indians and country while we were together. He's a good man, but not to be trusted around women. Seems like ever' time we came on a band of Indians, Crow, Shoshoni, or others, they all knew about him and there was usually at least one woman that claimed him." He chuckled at the memory, "And, when we came to the

Shoshoni, he was surprised he had a son. I think that's what made him stay with them, he was kinda proud of his offspring."

The trail hugged the low foothills of the Wind River range, rolling ridges that stretched out like boney fingers from the granite peaks and pointed to the valley of the Wind River that wound its way from the runoffs of the mountains. With the up and down of the trail that traversed ravine, finger ridge, ravine, the horses were showing weariness and Tate searched the trees for a camp site. After dropping off a ridge and coming to a narrow, willow-lined stream, Tate motioned to a shoulder clearing with tall grass and several aspen.

When they reined up at the clearing, Sadie spoke up, "Finally!" as she slipped from her saddle and dropped to the ground, calling Indigo to her side. "Come on, Indy, let's go get some firewood!"

The others stepped to their camp chores, with Sean gathering rocks for a fire ring, Tate unsaddling and hobbling the horses, and Maggie digging out the makings for supper. With several days on the trail, the camp routine had become familiar and each willing to do their share. Tate lifted his eyes to the tall mountains behind them, already showing the shadows of twilight, and knew darkness would soon drop its blanket on the mountainsides. They were all enjoying the expedition and it was good to have this journey of discovery together.

CHAPTER TWO
TRAIL

TATE GREETED THE FIRST LIGHT OF MORNING FROM ATOP THE ridge above their camp. As was his habit, he chose to spend the first moments of the day in communion with his Lord, and he sat with his back to the ridgetop as he faced east. He was reminded that many of the native peoples believed the sun was the personification of the Great Spirit, but he saw it as the handiwork of God. He had finished his prayer time and was enjoying the slow painting of the eastern sky when he saw Maggie climbing the loose-soiled slope to join him. As she neared, she turned to look back over her shoulder, "Looks like it's gonna be another beautiful day!"

"Looks like," answered Tate as he scooted aside to afford Maggie room on the flat rock he used for his seat. "I think we'll drop down into the valley today." He pointed to the north, "That's the Absaroka range, and where it peters out yonder, those little'uns are the Owl Creek mountains or hills. But they point right into the Crow territory. Course, all that yonder," pointing north and northwest up the valley of the Wind River, "was allotted to the Crow with that treaty at

Fort Laramie back in '51, but most of 'em are still fightin' about it."

"I thought we were goin' to the Shoshoni country?"

"We are, that's mostly on the other side of the Wind River mountains and farther north, but they weren't part of the treaty, so they claim more of the north country. But then again, so do the Blackfeet. Course, before the white man came, none of 'em had boundaries. They just claimed certain areas as their hunting grounds and fought anybody that didn't agree."

"Well, this place you've talked about so much, what'd you call it? The land of wonders and waters? Whose land is that?"

"Hard tellin', from what I heard it wasn't part of the treaty, but I s'pose whoever's there, claims it. But, most of 'em kinda see it as a place of spirits, and they don't like it too much."

"So, how long is it gonna take us to get there?"

"Oh, mebbe 'nother week, or so," grinned Tate as he slipped his arm around Maggie's waist to pull her closer.

"A week?! We've already been travelin' a week, and you're tellin' me another week?" She pushed away from him to look directly into his eyes, daring him to use his usual tactic of silence.

"That's why we took off so early in the spring, so's we'd have all the time we needed. 'Sides, you're enjoyin' it, ain'tcha?" he pulled her close again.

Maggie dropped her chin to her chest and softly admitted, "Yes. We haven't traveled like this since our first time together. I've missed it."

He put his fingertips to her chin to tip her face toward him and savoring the beauty of his wife, especially with the reflected colors of the rising sun that had painted the half dome of the sky with all the shades of pink and orange, and now highlighted the angel kisses on her face. He bent and kissed her as she wrapped her arms around his neck and pulled him close.

As they separated, he said, "We better go down and get the kids rousted out, or we might not make it in a week."

She giggled at him and stood to lead the way down the hill to their camp.

TATE HAD a way about him that made it easy for him to befriend many of the native peoples. As a youth, his best friend was a part of the Osage, and when he was still in his teens and making his way to the Rockies, he made friends with the Kiowa and Comanche. While living in the Sangre de Cristo's, he befriended different bands of the Ute, and gained the respect of the Jicarilla Apache. His first wife was of the Arapaho, and his good friend acquainted him with the Shoshoni, or Snake. His first meeting with the mountain Crow was friendly, but his encounters with the other bands of the Crow had been bloody. Now they were in Crow country and bound for the land of the Blackfeet, who were not known to be too friendly with whites. But he knew enough that, no matter whose land he was in, or thought he was in, to not take any chances, because every tribe had their renegades and outcasts that would gladly take the scalp of any white man or woman.

By mid-morning, they had crossed the bald knob of a finger ridge that stretched out from the tall peaks of the Wind River range and started for a game trail that followed a dry creek bed in the bottom of a long ravine that promised to take them into the valley below. The timber was thick with droopy-armed fir and towering spruce, and the bottom of the ravine held a smattering of aspen that shook their fresh green leaves at the passersby. The morning breeze came from the valley and danced its way toward the granite peaks, whispering through the pines and carrying the fragrance of pine needles blended with larkspur, chickweed and sego lily.

Sean had pestered his father repeatedly, begging to take the lead on the trail and Tate finally relented, knowing Sadie would have to be close behind. But it was an easy trail and would soon break out of the timber as they neared the valley bottom and it didn't offer any special hazards. Lobo was in the lead with Indigo close at his side, but they would occasionally get a considerable distance ahead, sometimes even out of sight in the thick trees. Tate and Maggie followed behind but staying far enough back to give the youngsters their sense of independence and freedom. The packhorses, a dapple-grey and a leopard appaloosa, were on long leads behind Maggie and Tate.

When the trail rounded a slight knob, Tate stood in his stirrups to look through the timber to the valley below and was startled by a shout from Sean and a squeal from their horses. Tate dropped to his saddle and quickly kicked Shady to a fast trot to round the bend and see a melee before him. A black ball of fur was shinnying up a fat spruce on the uphill side of the trail, Lobo and Indigo were barreling their way back toward the youngsters, and Sean and Sadie were fighting to stay aboard their horses that were rearing and bucking and bouncing off one another in the middle of the trail. Tate saw at once the cause of the commotion was an upset momma black bear fighting her way to her cubs, one high up in the tree and the other clawing his way to join him.

Maggie rounded the knob just in time to see Tate swing down from his saddle as Shady, wide-eyed and bending in the middle, side-stepped away from the bear as if he were about to be clawed. Tate stumbled, caught his balance and brought up the rifle just as Maggie shouted, "NO! She's got cubs!" pointing to the tree. Tate spun to look at her, but the growling bear changed Tate's mind, and he turned to see the bear rise to her hind legs, open her mouth wider than Tate thought possible but instantly knew it was wide enough to take in his whole head. He grabbed for his Dragoon and shouted at the bear, lifted the pistol and fired over her head, once, twice, and on the third shot, the bear dropped to all fours and started for the same tree that held her cubs.

Tate looked to Sean, saw he had brought his horse under control as they were farther down the trail, looked to Sadie, just in time to see her topple from the paint and had his attention taken by Lobo and Indigo as they launched themselves off the trail toward the bear tree. Tate ran to Sadie to see if she was alright, but by the time he reached her side, she was standing and brushing herself off, watching her horse trot to the side of Sean and his Appaloosa.

"Go get your horse, and you two stay there!" Tate shouted, over the growling of bears and wolves. He spun around and saw Maggie, still aboard and with both lead ropes of the packhorses, leading them away from the ruckus and back up the trail. Shady stood, shaking beside the trail, looking at Tate, waiting for the commotion to subside. Tate looked at the tree, saw the Momma bear nearing her cubs and looking over her shoulder at the wolves below. He hollered to Sean and Sadie, "Go on down the trail, we'll catch up!" waving them downhill.

He walked back to Shady, speaking softly and picked up the reins, stepped in the stirrup and swung aboard, putting his Sharps in the scabbard in one smooth movement. He reined Shady around, stopped, looked back to the tree and whistled, calling, "Lobo! Indy! C'mon!" and motioned them to follow. Lobo looked at him, back up at the bear, dropped his front feet from the trunk of the cup holding tree and started to follow Tate. With one look over his shoulder and a low growl, he got Indigo's attention, and the black pup soon followed.

Maggie and Tate swung wide of the trail and cut across the dry creek bottom at a run, up the opposite slope and found another game trail that was barely in the trees to follow down the ravine and circle around and past the bear. From the sparse tree coverage, they had little trouble spotting the bear, now working her way down the tree and scolding her cubs all the while. And soon after, they saw the youngsters, now well down the trail and away from harm. Tate motioned them to cross over to their side and come along.

By the time they approached the tree line, Tate had spotted a likely campsite, and with a thick cover of quakies, they made camp for the night. Everyone was played out with all the excitement, but the conversation around their dinner plates was about the day's adventure.

Sean spoke with his mouth full, "Boy, Pa, when Sadie got dumped, I thought sure that ol' bear would come after us!"

"Me too! I was really scared!" added Sadie.

Maggie thought, but didn't express, *You were scared! I was terrified!'*

"Well, all of you did just fine. That's what you should always remember, if you keep your heads and do what you're told, things will work out for the best."

Maggie lowered her head, remembering the fear she felt for her children and the way her husband, as always, took control and made certain everyone was safe. This was a fearful country at times, but every place, even civilization, has its pitfalls and dangers. But with a man like Tate as their protector and leader, she felt as safe as she could, but yet there was always a nagging fear deep inside, the fear of a mother for her children and home. She breathed deep, trying to shake off the thoughts that troubled her, and smiled at her two youngsters, feeling that special pride that only a mother knows.

CHAPTER THREE

CALEB LAY WITH HANDS BEHIND HIS HEAD STARING AT THE stars in the black velvet night. This was the only time he didn't have someone barking orders at him and he reveled in the time of solitude. It was when he dared to dream, to think of his future and what his life might become. Born into slavery, Caleb spent the two decades of his life on old Mr. Winthrop's tobacco farm just west of St. Louis. The man had been a kindly owner, however, many of the overseers he employed through the years were not likeminded. But Caleb had been favored by the owner and often was chosen by Mr. Winthrop to do special tasks in and around the house. Occasionally, Caleb served as a driver for the master's carriage and had been schooled with three others, all house servants, to read and write, something they had to keep secret because Missouri law forbid the education of slaves. However, Mr. Winthrop wanted his chosen few to be able to converse intelligently and clearly and to even share their ideas regarding the farm and home. Caleb had even been allowed to take Beatrice, his life-long friend and sweetheart, as a wife.

As he lay on the deck of the side-wheeler riverboat, *St.*

Mary, he remembered the last days on the farm. Mr. Winthrop had called him and Beatrice into the side room he called his office and showed him some papers, "You know what these are, Caleb?" holding the papers in front of him.

"Uh, no suh, I shore'nuff don't know, Massuh Winthrop. What do they be?"

"Oh, don't go talkin' that slave talk with me, you know better. These are the manumission papers for you and Beatrice, there. Now, they won't be any good till after I die, but just for your own knowin', they will be in this drawer," he motioned to the right-hand drawer of his desk. "I wanted you to know, because I've been feelin' poorly lately, an' the doctor doesn't have anything good to say 'bout my chances of livin' much longer."

Beatrice put her hand to her mouth and Caleb leaned forward, "But Mr. Winthrop, sir, you don't look poorly!" Both were alarmed at the news and had not expected either the report of his failing health nor the possibility of being set free. "What is it that ails you, sir?"

The old man coughed, holding an embroidered handkerchief to his mouth, and as he withdrew the hanky, he looked at and showed the spots of blood to the two. "Consumption, that's what he called it. Said it'll take me soon enough but can't be soon enough for me. Don't wanna live like this, can't hardly breathe!" He looked up at the pair that had served him all their lives and said, "You've been provided for in my will, and the others as well, but you two are to be set free with these papers. Keep 'em with you always, for there are others who won't agree with what I've done. That's why I want you to know where these are kept. Do you understand?"

"I think so, sir," answered Caleb, somewhat stunned by the news. He looked to Beatrice who stood with wide eyes of wonder but was silent.

. . .

IT WASN'T EVEN a week later when the overseer, Rafe Lafferty, called all the slaves together in front of the big house and announced, "Mr. Winthrop is dead." The overseer looked at the reactions of the many faces before him, reveling in the knowledge he would now be in charge and would not be limited by Winthrop. The owner had seventeen slaves including the house servants and Caleb, and most were surprised at the news. "Now, some o' you been thinkin' that Mr. Winthrop was gonna set you free with his will when he died, but that ain't so! Ain't none o' you gonna be set free nohow! Mr. Winthrop has a step-son that's gonna inherit ever'thing, you included, and he's keepin' me on as overseer! So, you just get those foolish notions outta your heads, cuz ain't none o' you goin' free!"

Beatrice looked to Caleb and he shook his head slightly to stay any reaction of his wife. She recognized the stern expression and knew they would talk about it later when they were alone, but she wasn't surprised that the dream of freedom had been stolen from them. It was a something she never thought would be possible and the brief time they shared together talking about freedom was more of a dream than they ever imagined. But she knew Caleb and believed he would not give up easily.

Since the overseer had moved himself into the big house, he demanded the servants treat him the same as the owner and he took his meals at the owner's table, at least until, or if, the new owner said different. But the step-son wasn't due for over a month.

Beatrice was to keep the overseer away from the office while Caleb retrieved their papers, but the chair squeaked when Caleb sat down to pull the drawer open and alarmed the overseer. When Lafferty stormed into the office and saw Caleb at the desk he shouted, "Git away from thar, boy!" as he waved a fist at Caleb.

With wide-eyed astonishment and determination, Caleb grabbed at the drawer and jerked it open, snatching up the papers.

"I said git back!" stormed Lafferty as he charged toward the man. There had always been a barrier of antagonism between the two and the overseer saw anyone that didn't kowtow before him as a belligerent slave that needed to be whipped.

"No suh! These papers belong to us!"

The overseer glared at the man behind the desk, looked around the room quickly for anything to use as a weapon and snatched up a candle stick, lifting it high and threatening. "Put them back 'fore I split yore skull!" he screamed.

"No suh! Ain't gonna do it!"

Lafferty swung at Caleb, but the slave stepped back, and the bronze candle stick whispered within inches of his head, causing the overseer to stumble and hit the desk, trip over his own feet and fall to the floor, striking his head on the hardwood, knocking him unconscious. The yelling had attracted the other servants of the house and Beatrice was the first into the office and witnessed the overseer try to strike her man. She screamed when Lafferty swung the candlestick, and gasped when he fell to the floor.

She looked up at Caleb, who stood frozen with the papers clasped in his hands to his chest. Caleb leaned over the corner of the desk to see the inert form of the overseer. The man was still breathing and Caleb looked back to his wife. She asked, "Is he . . . "

"No, he's still breathing. But when he wakes up . . . he'll wanna take the whip to me, for sure! I ain't gonna let no man whip me again, ever!" he spat as he shook his head. He looked directly at Beatrice, "Go, get your stuff together, we're leaving, tonight!"

. . .

CALEB DREW his knees up and sat up to lean against the rail and looked to the top deck where he knew Beatrice was working in the kitchen as a cook's helper. During the brief week when they dreamed about freedom, they talked about getting a job on one of the many riverboats that stopped at Mr. Winthrop's dock on the Missouri river to take on wood. The overseer made certain there was always plenty of wood at the dock for the river traffic as many of the captains paid for the wood in cash and it was well known among the slaves that the overseer always kept a portion for himself.

After their confrontation with the overseer, Caleb and Beatrice took their papers, the small satchel of coins he found with the papers, and their few personal belongings and traveled upstream of the Missouri to a likely stopping place where they might board a riverboat. They had taken a mule from the farm, intending to set it free knowing it would return of its own accord to the farm, and made good time as they fled from their life-long home. The very next evening, they found a riverboat tied up at the shore and the crew cutting firewood and hauling it aboard. When Caleb approached the obvious boss to ask for a job, the man looked at him and asked, "You a slave?"

Caleb reached in his shirt and brought out the papers and answered, "No suh! We are free, and muh wife would be a big help in the galley, she's a mighty fine cook!"

The man, who Caleb would later learn was one of the engineers, stepped forward and looked at him. "Well, you look like you could do some work." He poked at Caleb with what appeared to be a walking stick. What he saw was a man close to six feet tall, broad shouldered with bulbous muscles that told of years of heavy work, and a tapered torso to thickly muscled legs that stretched the canvas britches tight. Caleb weighed what Mr. Winthrop called 16 stone, or 225 pounds, all muscle.

Caleb stepped back when the man poked at him with his stick but didn't shy away from the contact as he looked at the man with a blank expression.

The man turned to shout at the upper deck, "Yo, Steward!"

A man stepped from the doorway midship and hollered back, "What!" as he wiped his hands on a dirty rag.

"You need a cook's helper? I got a woman here that wants a job!"

"Send her up! Mebbe she can do better'n Cooky! 'Bout time we got some good food 'roundchere!"

The engineer looked back at Caleb, "Send her up! An' you, take your gear, stow it yonder," as he pointed to the aft portion of the ship, "an' git back here and haul wood!"

That had been just over a week back, and the routine of the work as a roustabout had kept him busy all the daylight hours and many of the hours of darkness. He had only visited with Beatrice a few short moments each day, as she had to bunk with the two women chambermaids, so they saw little of one another. But the work was easy after the years of labor Caleb had known, and times such as now on the deck, had been enjoyable. The crew had finished loading the firewood for the boiler and Caleb had taken a dip in the river before taking his place on the deck. There were several passengers who made their beds among the cargo for a cheaper fare and he met some of them, trappers, traders, and others, but he enjoyed the times of solitude.

He heard some of the buckskin-clad men talk of the mountains and their time of trapping and exploring and the talk stirred his thoughts of freedom and wandering without restraints. It was a pleasant thought, but it probably wouldn't be suitable for a man with a wife. But maybe there would be other things or places they could go together. They had been together all their lives, and they shared this wonderful dream of freedom. They would find something, surely.

AFTER DROPPING FROM THE HIGH-UP TRAIL IN THE BLACK timber on the shoulder of the granite peaks, their chosen trail followed the winding Wind River through the valley bottom. Sean had once again taken the lead after his father ribbed him, "Since there ain't no trees for bear cubs, why don't you take the lead son?"

"It'd be my luck for a stray cub to come runnin' away from his ma and start the ruckus all over, even if there ain't no trees!"

"I'll take the lead, Pa!" piped up Sadie, anxious to show how daring she was even at the tender age of seven going on eight.

"Well, since we're in open country, how 'bout the two of you ridin' together?" Tate looked down at Lobo and Indigo and ordered, "An' you two try to keep 'em outta trouble!" motioning them to take the trail ahead. He knew the wolves would provide fair warning of any danger without fail, even though the last escapade came from the thick timber after they had passed, it was more of a fluke with the pup distracting the ever-watchful Lobo. Tate looked to Maggie and grinned, "They're sure tryin' to grow up fast, ain't they?"

"Sometimes I wonder if they're tryin' or you're pushin'!" declared the redhead as she tugged on the lead rope of the spotted packhorse.

"That's the best way to learn, gettin' out there an' doin' it!" answered Tate as he pointed the mouse colored grulla gelding to the trail. "Come on Shady, you understand, don't you?" and reached down to pat his horse on the neck. As he straightened up he lifted his eyes to the sky, saw thick clouds with dark bottoms, forming along the granite peaks on both sides of the valley. "Might be in for a bit of a storm after a spell," he commented, as he looked back at Maggie.

"Think we can find cover 'fore it hits?" asked the redhead.

"Prob'ly. We'll need to keep an eye on it, though. This wagon road'll be easy goin' an' as long as we stay away from them washes an' ravines, we'll find us a place with some good timber after a spell."

This was the second day in the valley bottom. They camped last night where the Wind River made a sharp turn back on itself after carving a horseshoe bowl from the tall clay and sandstone hillside, leaving jagged rock formations that resembled ogres and goblins keeping watch over the river below. Everyone commented on the formations and Sadie shivered as she said, "They look like evil monsters hanging up there!"

With most of the feeder creeks coming from the towering Wind River mountains, the dry foothills on the east side of the river held little vegetation, aside from the usual cholla, prickly pear, yucca, and bunch grass. With the wagon road carved by early frontier traders heading to rendezvous across the mountains, it was easy going for the Saint family. But Tate was concerned about the coming storm, knowing the cloudbursts and flash floods were more dangerous than any imagined monsters or real animals of the wilderness.

They were on a bald knob overlooking the river bottom when Tate saw a distant flash of lightning farther up the valley and nearer the mountains. He waited, counting to himself, and when the thunder rattled the heavens, he knew they should be looking for shelter. He stood in the stirrups and scanned the valley bottom and the nearby foothills, leaning side to side to search for a campsite. He saw familiar landmarks. Off his left shoulder and behind them rose some white-chalk cliffs over a narrow canyon, and directly to his left stood a tall timber covered mountain. In the distance, he saw a narrowing of the valley where the river cut its way through a sandy finger slope, and beyond were tree covered foothills.

He motioned Sean to wait and rode up beside him. He pointed out the cut of the river and said, "Just beyond that notch, this wagon road turns back toward the mountain. That's the Union Pass that ol' Bridger found. We'll make camp at the foot of that pass, an' we might need to pick up the pace a mite, that storm's workin' its way back t'ward us."

"Alright Pa, we'll do it!" answered the boy and gigged his horse forward with Sadie hot on his tail. They started at a trot but stepped it up to an easy lope and a grinning Tate and Maggie were straining at the lead ropes of the packhorses to keep up. They took the low hills above the river that made its S curve through the cut, and as they dropped off the last small rise, Sean led the way to splash through the shallow river, now no more than a creek, and into the narrow meadow beyond. He made for the black timber that marked the edge of the rising mountain and reined up in the lee of the trees to await the others.

When Tate and Maggie stopped beside Sean, the boy

asked, "This alright, Pa?" and motioned to the trees behind him.

Tate scanned the trees, saw a slight shoulder higher up and pointed it out, "Let's head to that shoulder. It'll be a little more protected and there's plenty of trees for what we need."

Sean looked, and started his Appaloosa into the trees, picking his way through the ponderosa and spruce. The shoulder was open to the sky, but the sunlight was dimmed by the heavy clouds that appeared to be huddling overhead. Once everyone was in the small clearing, Tate dropped to the ground and began giving each one instructions for the camp.

"Sadie, you start gathering firewood and help your mother get a fire going. Sean, help me picket the horses and get the gear together."

Everyone quickly set about their tasks and Tate and Sean were soon erecting a shelter between a couple of big spruce. With a long pole lashed to lower branches of the trees, they began stacking long branches into a lean-to form for both their shelter and a windbreak for the horses. They soon had an adequate shelter made and they rolled out the bedrolls on the ground covers.

The women had prepared the meal of strip steaks broiled over the fire, some baked camas bulbs, and hot coffee. As they ate, the thunder rattled the rocks and trees around them, threatening to let loose the dogs of storm and everyone hastened their eating, looking to the inviting bedrolls under the protection of the pine bough lean-to. The horses were restless, and pushed into their shelter, and close to one another.

The rain came suddenly and with huge drops that splattered on the rocks and soon doused the fire. The family was sitting in the shelter and watched as the boughs of the ponderosa and its long needles bent with the downpour. The puffing and snapping of the fire and coals protested the water but the blackened logs and grey ashes were soon drowned into a puddle of blackwater. The horses had settled down, knowing they had to endure the deluge but were thankful for the shelter. The wind tried pushing the torrent to the side, but the water came with relentless force and soon rivulets snaked through the trees, carrying pine needles down the sloping hillside.

Jagged white lances stabbed at the far mountain and the roar of cascading floodwaters began. Thunder boomed overhead and was felt in the ground beneath the campers. Sadie huddled close under her mother's arm, and Sean leaned toward his pa. Lobo and Indy had crawled into the shelter and lay alongside the youngsters. Every time the swords of lightning crackled, all six occupants of the lean-to jerked involuntarily, and each one let slip an exclamation or a nervous chuckle.

Off to the southeast could be heard the growing calamity of a flash flood forcing its way down a ravine cluttered with rock and brush, never yielding and always pushing, until the roar of rapids rivaled the booming thunder. Maggie lifted Sadie to seat her between her and the girl's Pa. Tate pulled Sean closer and the wolves whimpered jealously. There was no sleeping with all the noise and no conversation with all the commotion. What few words were passed were in response to a plaintive cry from Sadie or a question from Sean, and then the answers came in a shout, just to be heard.

Suddenly, an explosion of sound and force shook the ground beneath them and each one jerked and shouted. Sadie started crying and Sean grabbed at his pa. Lobo and Indigo had jumped to their feet, looking out and into the trees. The slow crackling that sounded like rifle fire increased, and a crashing like thunder ripped through the trees and a sudden thud with branches splitting told Tate lightning had just downed a giant of the forest. "It's alright, lightning just struck a tree and it fell over. It was uphill and away from us so everything's alright."

"Lightning struck a tree?" whimpered Sadie.

"That's right, it struck a tree."

"Could lightning strike these trees?" she asked, trembling and pointing to the two nearby trees that held up the shelter.

"Well, I s'pose, but lightning usually strikes the tallest thing around. And I made sure there were other trees nearby that were taller than these two, so I don't think we have anything to worry about." He reached down and patted Sadie on her knee, reassuring her by his touch and presence.

Maggie looked at him with a frown that was as much a question as anything and Tate knew she was wondering if what he said was true. He shrugged his shoulders to her, because he didn't know it to be true, it was just one of those things he had heard some of the other mountain men say and it seemed logical. But, in the mountains, nothing was certain, and everything was suspect, even the wisdom of the explorers. But at this time, there wasn't much else to do but just wait out the storm and perhaps spend a little time praying.

CHAPTER FIVE
BUCKSKINNERS

"You sound like an educated man when you want to, have you any education?" asked the buckskinner, known as the Professor, speaking to Caleb as the two stood by the rail before the churning sidewheel of the riverboat.

"Mr. Winthrop, the owner of the farm, had a few of us chosen ones into the house and he saw to our education. He taught us to read, write, do sums, and more. He said he wanted us to speak well and share ideas about things. My wife, she works in the galley on board, and I both were educated by the master," explained Caleb, speaking as soft as possible with the splashing of the sidewheel making their conversation difficult.

"But, I thought you were a free man," queried the grey-haired man as he stroked his neatly trimmed Vandyke whiskers with one hand and held to the railing with the other.

"We are. Mr. Winthrop gave us our manumission papers before we left the farm. We both wanted to see the mountains and experience the freedom of the wilderness, so, we took jobs on the riverboat," explained Caleb, then changed the subject with a question. "Why do they," with a nod toward the other buckskinners that the man was traveling with, "call you Perfesser? Are you like a teacher?"

The older man chuckled, "No, no I'm not. But because I don't often speak with the vernacular of the mountain man and because I'm well-read and talk about books and such, they like to think I was a professor in some college. But I wasn't, however, that's a different tale. It's not considered good manners to ask a man about his previous life before the mountains. I have found men come from all walks of life. I've known some to be highly educated and well-to-do, others with a history of bad behavior, murders and such, while some were farmers, tradesmen, outlaws, runaways, what have you. But out here, a man's past is his own affair and folks judge a man by his deeds and behavior here. It's a good way. I believe every man should have a fresh start now and then."

"That's a good thought, but not everyone believes that," remarked Caleb, wistfully.

"What about you, Caleb? Once we get to Fort Union or on to Fort Benton, are you and your wife returning with the boat, or . . . "

"We don't want to go back, but I just don't know what to do or how to do it when we reach the end of the line. From what I hear, there's lots of Indians there, is that true?"

The portly man chuckled as he looked to this greenhorn and said, "Well, let me see. There's Assiniboine, Sioux, Blackfeet, Crow, Mandan, Hidatsa, and Arikara and a few others at times. So, yes, there are Indians. But it's a mighty big country and once away from the trading posts, we don't see 'em all that often." He paused as he looked somewhat critically at the man before him. Caleb was an impressive figure with broad shoulders and bulging muscles built with hard labor, and Professor was considering. "Have you ever thought about going to the mountains, like we are," with a sweeping hand toward his friends, "trapping, hunting, and such. We've done alright for ourselves, but the beaver trade has pretty well dried up, so this trip we're going for more pelts like bear, cougar, and such. But we could use a man that could handle himself and tend to camp duties like bundlin' hides and such. Interested?"

Caleb's eyes grew wide and he looked at the man's expression attempting to determine if the man's offer was genuine, "I might be, but what about my wife?"

Professor chuckled, "I don't think any of the men would object to having a woman doing the cooking. We've had enough of our camp cooking to last a lifetime. And, we'd teach you all you need to know about living in the mountains!"

Caleb let a grin cross his face and leaned back from the rail as he looked at the man, "That sounds fine. I'll be talking to my wife soon and I'll let you know for sure, if that's alright."

The men parted with Caleb excitedly taking the steps to the top deck two at a time. Professor observed the big man leave and turned to his friends that were lounging on the bales of cargo and watching him approach.

"So Perfesser, what'chu been talkin' 'bout wit' that big slave? Me'n the boys here been wonderin' what a educated man like you could have to talk 'bout with a ignorant slave?" asked the one known as Curly. His bushy eyebrows, sideburns, and chin whiskers were an attempt to overcome his lack of anything atop his head. Although he appeared to be naturally bald, the wrinkled skin, whiter than the rest of his pate, told the story of scalping. It happened long before he joined with his current partners and the topic was one to be avoided. He never talked about his experience, but they knew he had a hatred for all Indians.

Professor looked at the questioner, "I convinced him to come with us and be our camp helper! And before you get all riled up about it, he's bringing his wife also!"

The three men stared, aghast. The idea of bringing a slave and a woman with them into the mountains and Indian country was unconscionable. It was all most trappers could do to protect themselves, much less a greenhorn and a woman. Curly started to object but met the upraised hand of Professor, "His wife is a fine cook! She's working in the galley and fixing that fine food for the fancy pants people in the cabins," nodding to the upper deck. "And I figger we could use some good cooking and a big man like that to bundle the pelts. With them doin' all that work, we could spend more time huntin' and trappin'!"

Smitty, the biggest man of the group and also the dirtiest and most vulgar, stood up and walked closer to Professor, "Do we hafta keep 'em fer the whole trip?" implying any number of possible misdeeds.

"Well, if something was to happen to them along the way, I don't know who would miss them, do you?" answered the grinning Professor.

Smitty and Curly looked to one another and slowly grinned, but the fourth member of their party, Long Tom, stood quietly leaning on a cargo box and stared at his companions. Long Tom was not a man of many words, most often choosing silence and solitude, but the black eyebrows shaded his squinty eyes as he turned and walked away.

THE CARGO BOXES and bundles were stacked on one side and the stalls with horses and mules were on the opposite with a narrow passageway between the two. Caleb was at the end of a long handled, flat-bladed shovel he was using to scrape the manure from the deck. He stood to stretch his back and looked to the bills of lading glued to the boxes. There were boxes of knives, showing 1100 scalping knives, 124 dozen knives, and 300 tomahawks. Another bill showed 1200 half axes, 60 felling axes, 100 battle axes. A large bundle held 112 pairs of blankets, bolts of fabrics, 300 mirrors. Other boxes told of hoes, buttons, beads, vermillion and verdigris. And at the bottom of the stack were the many boxes and barrels of gunpowder, lead, tobacco and liquor, purposely put there to prevent any pilfering.

Caleb bent back to his work, scraping and shoveling and finally using buckets of river water to swamp the deck clean of any other debris. As he finished up, the big buckskinner, Smitty, approached and spoke, "So, you might be comin' along wit' us, eh?" He stuck his thumbs under his galluses atop his dirty Linsey Woolsey shirt and with one eye cocked he looked at Caleb. Although Smitty was a big man, his size was more to bulk than brawn. But Caleb stood at least a half-hand taller and his shoulders broader.

"Thinkin' on it," answered Caleb, resorting to his usual slave vernacular whenever around strangers. Many whites were offended when a slave spoke better and would accuse the black man of being uppity.

"So, this wife o' your'n, she good lookin'?"

Caleb reached for the shovel leaning against the cargo boxes before answering, "Muh woman's a good cook, 's'all that matters."

Smitty started to retort but caught himself as he looked at the big man with the shovel at his side. He grunted and nodded as he turned away, with a bit of a scowl on his face and evil in his eyes. He grinned to Curly as he returned to his chosen spot atop a long bundle of cargo. The expressions were seen by Long Tom and the tall thin quiet man glanced to Caleb, wondering.

CHAPTER SIX
BLACKFEET

THE PIIKÁNI OR PEIGAN BANDS OF THE NIITSITAPI OR Blackfeet confederacy had gathered for a spring buffalo hunt and a council of chiefs had been called to meet together in the lodge of Nee-ti-nee or Lame Bull. Seated around the center circle were Lame Bull, Mountain Chief, Low Horn, Little Gray Head, Big Snake, The Skunk, and Middle Sitter. These respected leaders and elders of the Peigans were somber and quiet as they waited for Lame Bull to speak. The old chief waited for other leaders and warriors to be seated in the outer circles, usually according to rank or position within the band, but once all were still and attentive, he searched the circles for one warrior known as Banni Sanglant. When he spotted the warrior, he began. "It is good to have our brothers join us for our buffalo hunt, and you are welcome," he paused as mumbled greetings and agreements were made among those present. "But I am saddened at the word received for the loss of our brother," he refrained from speaking the name of the dead warrior, as was the custom, but all knew to whom he referred.

Lame Bull stood before continuing, "It is the custom of the people that anyone may leave a band and join himself with another at any time. And it is believed that no one can tell another what he can or cannot do, he must answer to Manitou or the Great Spirit. But for the protection of our people, there are times that certain deeds must be punished and in the worst times, we must cast out a member. It is with heavy heart that I speak of such a man today.

"When this one was born to the French trapper, LaPer-riere, and the woman of our village, Walks Alone, his father named him Banni Sanglant. He was accepted by our people as one of us and he grew together with our young men to become a warrior. He went on raids with our fighting men, was of the Running Wolves Warrior society, and counted many coups. But he also took scalps of those he did not kill and claimed them as his own, even when the warrior who made the kill faced him. This he did three times.

"Our warriors returned from a raid against the Shoshoni, and this time he did more." The chief looked to the leader of the warrior society that made the attack and motioned for him to stand and tell of the raid. Little Dog was seated in the second circle and stood to face the leaders.

"Before we attacked the keepers of the horse herds, I told each warrior of his duty, and knowing Banni and his way, I pulled him aside to give his orders. He agreed, and we began our attack. Banni and the one that died had been friends since they were young and they were to attack together. But Banni did not do as told, and the one that died made a kill of a Shoshoni. Banni claimed the kill and the two fought. Banni killed his friend and took his scalp and the scalp of the Shoshoni," this remark brought shouted exclamations from the group, anger expressed with hoots and beating on the ground. Little Dog continued, "And Banni claimed the

Shoshoni had killed his friend and he took the scalp of the killer, but he was seen by me and Bear Robe and Little Red Buffalo."

All of those in the lodge turned to look at the mentioned warriors who sat with stoic expressions, nodding their heads in agreement with the speaker. Low Horn, seated to the left of the chief Lame Bull raised his hand with open palm before the circle, signaling for silence. He turned to face Lame Bull, "This Banni is a part of your band?"

Lame Bull nodded his head as he answered, "He is."

"Has he been trouble before this?"

"Yes, for the taking of other warriors prize, as Little Dog said."

Low Horn looked to Banni Sanglant and asked, "Did you have a dispute with the one that died before this?"

"No," came the simple answer from the scowling Banni.

Little Dog stood again, looked to Banni and spoke to the circle, "This man and the one that died had fought often about the woman, Star Shield. She wanted to be the woman of the one that died, but Banni wanted her."

The men of the lodge looked at one another, understanding more about the man Banni.

Lame Bull looked around the circles, waiting for any other speakers and seeing none, directed himself to Banni. "There are many things that are wrong with what has been done. As Little Dog has spoken, you have killed one of our own. You have not told truth when you said a Shoshoni killed him. When you took his scalp was the worst, you have brought shame upon our people and wronged the dead. These are to be punished by word of the council. You heard me say no man can tell another what he can do, but as a council for our people, we must act for the people and their good. But you now may speak to the council, if you wish."

Banni Sanglant looked at the chief, then stood to his feet. He scowled at each one, balled his fists angrily, breathed deep through his nose as he ground his teeth, and began. "From the time I was old enough to know, many of you," he pointed around the circle in a sweeping motion, "would have nothing to do with me or my mother because she had become the squaw of a white man. But I fought each one to prove I was one of you. The white man has been our enemy, the Crow and Shoshoni have been our enemy. But now you!" he shouted and pointed at Lame Bull, "and these," motioning toward the other leaders, "talk about making a treaty with the white man and let the Crow and Shoshoni have our lands and let the white men and our enemies hunt on our lands and you will not fight them! If you ban me, I will still fight the white man and our enemies until they are no more or until I cross over! I am Banni Sanglant, a warrior of the Running Wolves society! But if I am no more a part of this band, I will have my own band and we will be known as the Bloody Outcasts!" He seated himself with a grunt, knowing his very name, Banni Sanglant, given to him by his French father when he was but a boy, meant Bloody Outcast, as his father thought he would certainly become just that.

Lame Bull looked around the circle of leaders and directed, "If you say this man must be banished from our people, turn your back to him. If you believe he should stay with the people, remain as you are."

Each of the leaders looked to Lame Bull and to one another. Low Horn dropped his eyes to the ground, the muscles in his jaw working as he gritted his teeth in anger, then placing his hands on the floor of the lodge, he rose to his knees, turned around with his back to the center of the circle and sat down. One by one, every member of the inner circle of leaders and elders did exactly as Low Horn. When the last one facing Banni was Lame Bull, the chief said, "You will go to the lodge of your mother, take your things from the lodge and your horses from the herd and leave before the sun is gone." Then Lame Bull turned his back and the leaders sat in silence as all the warriors left the lodge, no one speaking to or looking at Banni Sanglant.

As is true in any small village, Walks Alone heard the verdict of the council before Banni returned. As he entered, she looked up at her son, sorrowful eyes brimming with tears, "I am sorry, my son," and she stood to embrace him. He stepped to the side to reach for his belongings. He did not look at his mother nor did he answer. As he searched for his possessions, he cast aside robes and blankets, pouches and parfleches, mumbling and growling all the while. Walks Alone sat on her robe and watched the son that would soon leave her presence forever, and she let the tears slide unhindered down her cheeks, as she sat, unashamed and hurting.

Banni had assembled a pile of his buckskins, weapons and blankets and stood, finally looking at his mother. He dropped to the robe beside her, "You have been a good mother to me. It has been my anger at my father and toward others, that I could not control." He hit his knee with his fist, bit his lip and continued, "It is good that I go. When I am gone, perhaps Middle Sitter will finally do what he has wanted and come to you." He looked at his mother and grinned.

"I am not concerned with that man, it is you, my son, that I care about."

He touched her arm gently, looked at her and said, "There is nothing to be done. There are others like me, I will find them, and we will band together. Middle Sitter will be a good man for you." He stood and bundled his things together, picked up his bow and quiver, and started for the entry way. Walks Alone followed him out and both were surprised when they saw Banni's friend, Four Horns, seated on his horse, leading another that was loaded for traveling, and holding the leads of the two horses for Banni.

Banni looked to Four Horns, "What are you doing? You cannot be here."

"I will go with you. They," nodding his head toward the lodge of Lame Bull, "are wrong. I do not wish to stay with those who try to make peace with the white man or to let our enemies take our lands. I will go with you and we will fight together."

Banni looked at his friend, remembering that Four Horns had no family left. His entire family had fallen to the spotted disease of the white man when he was a small child. He had been raised as a waif of the people and passed from lodge to lodge. With a deep breath, Banni nodded his head to his friend, looked back to his mother, and loaded his gear on the horses. He swung aboard, bent down to embrace his mother one last time, and reined around to leave the village that had been his home all his life. No one looked at him, and all turned their backs as he approached. But the scorn they showed matched the contempt he felt as he dug his heels into the ribs of his mount, and together Banni Sanglant and Four Horns loped from the village, shouting their war cries in scorn.

The village was near the confluence of the two branches of the Musselshell River and Banni pointed his pony south. He knew the land held many white men, Shoshoni and Crow; all enemies of his people. He was determined to take his vengeance on those he had grown to hate and there were other villages of bands of the Piegans that would have warriors that would follow him as he made his war against their enemies. Although he could not approach their villages, Four Horns had not been banished from the people and he could easily find other disgruntled warriors that were eager for blood. Banni would build his band and show the cowardly leaders of the Piegans that he was the real warrior and killer of enemies.

IT WAS A WET CAMP THAT THE SAINT FAMILY FOUND WHEN they rolled from their blankets at first light. The drenching rain had showed no mercy to their gear, blankets, and entire encampment. When Tate sat up, he inadvertently hit the roof of the shelter with his head and caused all the accumulated moisture to bring another smattering of raindrops on the faces of the sleepers. That action was met with a chorus of complaints from everyone but Lobo and Indy, who quickly exited the lean-to to make their early exploration of the nearby woods. Tate had anticipated a wet camp and had covered some firewood and kindling in hopes of having enough for a warm fire to start the day. Within moments, he had a cook fire flaring and the crackling of the pitch in the pine wood brought everyone from their wet blankets to stand before the flames, hands outstretched to gain some warmth and attempt to dry out their clothes.

Tate and Sean stripped the branches from the lean-to and used the poles to fashion a frame to hang the blankets and clothing near the fire. Maggie put Sadie to work on the camas roots, yampa and onions, searing them to add to the simmering venison strips tended by Maggie. The coffee was perking, and the left-over cornbread was heating as Sean and Tate returned to the fire to await their morning fare.

"So, pa, where 'bouts we headin' this mornin'?" asked the ever-curious Sean, and by implication he was asking to lead the way.

Tate looked at his son and leaned back against the tree trunk. They had cleared the camp and scattered a good layer of the long dry ponderosa pine needles to keep everyone dry as they sat around the fire, cross-legged. "Well, I think I'm gonna take us up along the Wind a ways and then we'll cut up a draw that'll save us a couple miles and put us above the valley bottom and on dryer land. But, we'll be foller'in' the Wind till we get atop the Togwotee Pass. But I don't think that'll be till late today or even tomorrow."

"So, do ya think we'll see any unfriendlies today?"

"Here's how it is," he picked up a stick and brushed away the pine needles to make a sketch in the moist earth. "We're right here," he made an "X", "and from here thisaway," pointing to the east and south, "that's all Crow country." He made a line like a boundary, "and this here and back this-away," pointing to the south and west, "is Arapaho territory. And from here to the north and west is Shoshoni country. And the Wind River runs through most of it. 'Course, we could always run into Blackfeet just about anywhere." He sat back and looked at his son as he studied the scratching, "So, what do you think?"

"Well, we been friendly with the Arapaho, and you said the Shoshoni are peaceful, so I guess it's just the Crow and the Blackfeet we need to be concerned about," answered Sean, grinning as he sat back with his arms folded across his chest.

Tate chuckled as he looked at his son and cautioned, "Son, we may be friendly with the Arapaho and even the Shoshoni, but that doesn't mean all of them are friendly with us. And there's always the chance a raiding party of any tribe would attack, just because we're white men in their territory, and some of 'em don't like that!"

BY MID-MORNING, with Tate in the lead, the small party of travelers came to a bend in the Wind River that pointed to the north. Tate eyed the land before them that appeared as a giant alluvial mound from eons past that pushed the river away and had since been cut by run-off creeks that marred the work of the ages. He turned into the draw of a small creek, keeping their direction to the northwest and followed a game trail that crossed the slight slope of the mound. When the crooked creek bent back upon itself to the west, Tate pushed on toward the long ridge that came from the higher mountains. It was a ridge he knew would yield to the valley of the Wind River and would enable them to ride the higher trail above the valley bottom.

Scarcely an hour had passed from the time they left the river bottom and followed the creek that pointed them to the ridge, when Tate reined up and stepped down from the grulla. He slipped the Sharps from the scabbard and spoke to the others, "Step down and stretch your legs a little. I'm goin' to the crest yonder and eyeball the valley below. Sean, you come along." The boy gladly jumped down from his appaloosa and drew his Hawken from the scabbard to follow his pa. Tate motioned to Indy to stay and to Lobo to join them.

As they neared the crest, Tate went to all fours and approached the ridge slowly. He knew Sean would follow his example and he let a slight grin cross his face as he thought of the eagerness of his son to learn. Lobo was beside Tate as they dropped to their bellies and peered over the crest of the ridge, just above the saddle they would cross. When Sean came alongside, he spoke to him softly, "Now, search the valley below for any movement, but let your eyes keep moving. If you see anything, it will usually be when you're not looking directly at it."

The valley bottom was marked by the twisting Wind River that snaked its way toward the lower plains. Bounded on all sides with grassy flats and random clusters of willow and alder, the still pools of deep water reflected the blue sky and its few tufts of bright white clouds. The Rocky Mountains would often have one day of storms followed by clear blue skies and brilliant sunshine, as Tate and company enjoyed on this day. The sunshine warmed their backs as they scanned the valley and hillsides below.

"Look, Pa," spoke an excited Sean, pointing to a small herd of elk grazing beside the river. They numbered about fifteen and were leisurely foraging and enjoying the morning sunshine. By the sign, the animals had moved downstream along the river, and were heading to the lower end of the valley. They were about a quarter mile downstream from where Tate and Sean watched.

"I see 'em, son. But I don't think we need to be too concerned about 'em, we're not in need of meat and we don't have room to pack an entire elk along with us. Seen anything else?"

"Uh, no, just them elk."

"Let's take another good look, an' if there ain't nuthin' to worry 'bout, we'll get back on the trail," instructed Tate as he started his scan from the further most point toward the headwaters and moved his eyes along the river and hillsides back toward their perch. He glanced over to his son, waited for him to finish his look about and when the boy looked to his pa, he started to scoot back away from the crest. But just as Tate turned, a movement caught his eye. He rolled back to his belly and looked directly across the valley bottom to the far ridge above the white sided slope. As he looked, he heard a low growl from Lobo at his side. "Easy boy, I see 'em."

Sean had seen his father pause and roll back to look again and he did the same, curious at what had caught his father's attention. Coming from a notch in the steeper slope across the valley, that appeared as a cut from a runoff stream, was a string of mounted Indians. His father motioned with his hand for Sean to stay low and still as he reached for the telescope tucked in his belt at his back. Tate slowly brought it to his eye, shielding the end with his palm to prevent any reflection from the sun, and watched as the line of Indians reined up and were motioning toward the elk in the valley bottom. Tate whispered, "Crow!"

Sean looked and quietly asked, "How can you tell, pa?"

Tate dropped the scope and looked to his son, "Their hair and feathers. Many of the Crow grease their hair at the front, color it with vermillion or whatever they have, and make it stand up. They put their feathers in and point 'em to the side, where others have their hair layin' down and feathers stickin' up." He handed the scope to the boy, "Take a look, but hold your palm over the end of the scope like this," he demonstrated shielding the end, "to keep the sun off. When the bright sun hits that glass, it'll cause a reflection that they might see and know where we are."

"I see what'chu mean. But I don't see any paint. Does that mean they're just huntin'?"

"Prob'ly, but we won't take any chances. C'mon," he directed as he started to scoot back away from the crest and return to the horses and Maggie and Sadie.

When Maggie saw their approach, she asked, "You look like you saw something you don't like, what was it?"

"A Crow huntin' party. I think they're goin' after some elk we saw, but we should be able to avoid 'em. I was gonna take that saddle yonder," he turned to point out the dip in the ridge, "and drop back into the valley of the Wind, but we'll take that draw there where that creek comes down," he pointed to the draw that was the upper end of the one they followed to the mound. "It'll keep us behind the foothills and out of sight o' them Crow, and we can drop back into the valley a bit further up there. There will be plenty o' trees an' such and we'll be a long way from them."

He slipped his Sharps back into the scabbard and gestured or the others to mount up, so they could resume their trek. As he picked their way through the scrub oak brush on the hillside he thought back on the day and muttered a simple prayer of thanks to his Lord. He realized if they had stayed in their camp another day, as they considered, they would have been spotted by the Crow and might have been in for a fight. Or, if they had not seen the hunting party coming through the notch when they did, they would have been out in the open and seen by the hunters. Either situation could have been deadly, and he was thankful to his Lord for His protecting hand that guided their steps and their stops. He grinned at the thought, and said another "Thank you," just loud enough for Maggie to hear.

"What'd you say?" she asked, curiously.

"Oh, just thankin' the Lord for all He's done for us, that's all."

"Oh, I did too."

WITH THE LATER THAN usual start, they didn't stop for a midday break and meal but chose to put more distance between them and the Crow. With his chosen landmark that of a red slash atop a long ridge that pointed toward the pass, Tate kept his family on the trail that hugged the south side of the Wind River valley. It was easy going through the spruce, fir and ponderosa that covered the hillsides, but were not too thick to give way to the various game trails, paths that had been used by migrating elk and Indians alike. The gentle breeze that whispered through the pines coupled with the warm sunshine that was filtered by their branches, gave the family peaceful passage. They enjoyed the chiding calls of the whiskey jacks and scolds of the blue jays, the caw of the magpies and the screams of the circling osprey and eagles.

The sun had disappeared behind the treetops on the crests above them when Tate pointed Shady off the trail to a shoulder of a clearing at the edge of a spring fed creek that was well hidden in the cluster of spruce and aspen. It had been a long day, but an enjoyable one, and the family was anxious to take to their bedrolls for a good night's sleep in the warm and dry covers.

CHAPTER EIGHT
RECRUITING

BANNI SANGLANT AND FOUR HORNS SAT ON THEIR HORSES, watching a long line of villagers move across the flats before them. They were atop a rimrock bluff that stood sentinel over the valley and they did little to hide their presence. When they first spotted the village on the move, they were closer and had identified it as a Blood village, probably bound for the assembling of the bands for the celebratory Okan or Sun Dance. Now they watched as memories of past Okans tripped through their minds. The Sun Dance was the only gathering of the nations of the confederacy of the Niitsitapi or Blackfoot and was a time of celebration and planning. But Banni and Four Horns would never again be allowed to attend, and both men were pensive.

As they watched, four riders mounted the slope and trail that led to the top of the bluff and Banni knew they had been spotted. But he was not concerned, he saw this as an opportunity to get his message out among other bands and he sat taller as he watched them approach. When the riders recognized the two men as Piegan, they lowered their weapons and shields as they neared, but paused a considerable distance away. Banni and Four Horns were wearing war paint. Banni had painted the left half of his face black and the other side white. Jagged marks that resembled lightning could be seen at the sides of his bone breast-plate, and three feathers dangled at the back of his head. Four Horns was also painted, but his face was mostly white with a jagged streak of red crossing at an angle from above his right ear across his face and down his neck to the left shoulder. Similar designs and colors marked their horses.

"Ho!" greeted Banni as he raised his arm, palm forward, showing he was not an enemy.

The apparent leader of the four gigged his horse beside Banni's and looked suspiciously at the two men as he asked, "Do you hunt?"

"No, we are preparing for fighting our enemies."

At the word enemy, the four quickly looked around to see if others were present, and the leader asked, "And who are your enemies, I see no one."

"Our enemies are the same as your enemies, the Crow, the Shoshoni, and the many white men that would take our lands and kill our buffalo!" proclaimed Banni.

"What band are you from?" inquired the leader, as he squinted at the two, looking at their markings. Never before had he seen two men alone and painted for war when there were no others nearby.

"We were of Lame Bull's band, but no longer. He talks of signing a peace treaty with the whites who lie and he will not defend our lands! I am Banni Sanglant and we," motioning to Four Horns, "will start our own band of warriors! We will fight and drive these white men from our lands! Are there any among the Bloods who will join us? Or are you all becoming like the squaws of the Piegans?!" Banni was shouting his insults and invitation while his horse was prancing, being held in check by a tight rein.

Two of the warriors shouted their war cries in agreement with the words of the outcast, but the leader turned on them and stifled them with a scowl and an uplifted war axe. He spun back around and faced Banni, "Have you been banned?"

"Aiiieeee, we left because we could no longer stomach the cowardice of the leaders of our village! We had returned from a raid and I held two scalps from the Shoshoni, but the leaders said I was wrong for killing our enemy and taking his hair!"

Four Horns shouted his war cry and waved his lance in the air to show his stand with his friend. Horns had not been in the council lodge to hear the words spoken against Banni, but it would not have made any difference to the man; he was determined to make his mark as he followed his friend.

"You will not be at the Okan?" asked the leader.

"We go to find our enemies and take their scalps and all they have! We will soon have great numbers and many scalps, prizes, and honors! These are better things than food and dancing!"

For generations, the Sun Dance had been the most important day of the year for every one of the Blackfoot confederacy. A time when young men were admitted into warrior societies, men and women use the assembly as a time to find a mate, and families were reunited. For anyone to miss that time could only mean they were not allowed because of being an outcast. The leader of the four warriors, turned his back to the two and led his men from the bluff without another word or even a glance back at the rene-gades. Banni and Four Horns waved their lances and shields and shouted their war cries as the four dropped out of sight.

Banni looked to his friend, "We will see if there are any warriors among the Bloods. We will make our camp and let our fire be seen." It was nearing sundown and the villagers were starting to make their camp as well. Horns and Banni had gathered ample firewood and had a sizable blaze flaring, much larger than would ever be used for a camp, but it was a taunting signal to those camped below. And Banni was not to be disappointed. Within less than two hours of full dark, hoof beats were heard approaching on the trail. Five men, all painted for war, came to the fire, and one stepped forward, "I am Peenaquim, Seen From Afar, we are from the band of Buffalo Back Fat of the Bloods, and we have come to make war beside you!" At this remark, the other four men waved their lances or war clubs and shouted their war cries.

Before their cries died, two others stepped from the darkness and one spoke, "I am Red Crow of the Fish Eaters band of Two Suns, and we are here to make war beside you as well!" His companion shouted and was joined by the others as each chanted his war cry.

Banni stood and welcomed the newcomers, "It is good that you join us. We will take many scalps and honors as well as plunder. Come, we have much depuyer and pemmican to share and we will leave early to begin!"

———

IT WAS the 12th day out from Fort Union. Caleb and Beatrice had joined the buckskinners on the promise by the Professor of good treatment and ample supplies in exchange for Caleb's labors and Beatrice's cooking. The first six days were long and arduous travel, but the last five days they had been in the same camp and were told they would stay here for a week or more. The time had started well enough with the men being respectful of Beatrice and affable enough with Caleb, but once they established this camp, Caleb and Beatrice noticed a slight change in the men's manner.

"I'm telling you Caleb, I'm afraid. Especially of the one they call Smitty, and Curly isn't much better. It's all I can do to stay out of reach of that man!" Beatrice was leaning toward Caleb and speaking softly as the two gathered firewood. The only other man in the camp was the ever silent, Long Tom.

Caleb was known to be short-tempered and easily provoked to fight, but that was among the slaves. His only run-in with a white man was when the overseer tried to take their papers, and that was only a shove that caused the man to fall and strike his head. It wasn't like he had intentionally picked a fight with the man. But this was different, he was very protective of his wife and would never allow another man to put a hand on her, no matter what color of skin he might have. "I'll talk to Perfesser, maybe he can make them mind their manners."

"So help me, if they try to grab me, I'll pour hot coffee on 'em or somehin'! I'll not have them pawin' at me all the time. We came with them to work and cook and learn about the mountains, that's all!" she declared as she slammed a stick of wood onto the pile in Caleb's arms. "And if they gets to drinkin' you know that's what they'll do!"

"I'll not allow that!" snarled Caleb, nostrils flaring and a scowl disfiguring his face.

The other three had returned to the camp and Curly pulled the carcass of a black bear and its cub from a very skittish mule. All the horses and mules were jumpy at the presence of a bear, even though it was dead, just the smell made them nervous. Curly hollered to Caleb, "Hey boy! C'mere an' get this thang!" kicking at the carcass.

As Caleb neared, Smitty said, "We'll help ya git it strung up on the pole thar, an' you can start skinnin' it out. We gutted it and it shore did stink! But that thar pelt'll bring us some good money, both of 'em will. An' I got a lynx yonder. You can do it when you get done wit' them bear." He handed him a skinning knife, "An' be careful with that. I keep 'em sharp and if you cut them pelts, they won't be worth nuthin'," he declared, glaring at the big man. He had been intimidated by Caleb as the man stood several inches taller, was obviously more muscled and didn't cower like he was used to having slaves do around him, being a former overseer. He had told no one of his time in the field with slaves; he had been a vicious taskmaster and used the bull-whip to force his will on the field hands. But Caleb was a free man and had a penchant to stand up for himself and his wife and refused to knuckle under to the will of Smitty. Yet the vile white man was determined to have what he though was his due. The bear was quickly hung spread eagled, head down, from the cross bar, and Caleb picked up the knife and began his work. He had skinned animals before, but never a bear and he was startled at both the smell and the look of the creature. As he peeled the hide back, the carcass held an uncanny resemblance to that of a man.

Smitty turned away from Caleb and hollered, "Hey, Perfesser! How 'bout breakin' out some o' that corn likker?" and chuckled as he walked toward the fire. Beatrice was serving up the venison stew, made with skunk cabbage, deer meat, cat-tail root and onions.

With a cup of hot coffee in one hand and a tin plate in the other, the Professor answered, "Wait'll after supper!" and heard the grumbling complaint of Smitty as he came to the fire. "Three hides in the first couple days, and now these, that's a good start. I'm thinkin' we're gonna have a good season." The professor was making light conversation, but his remark went unanswered by the others. Long Tom had taken his plate and cup and sat a little apart from the others, but the professor knew that was his way and when he looked to the tall slender man, he heard no rejoinder from him either.

Curly finished his meal, tossed his plate aside, expecting

the woman to fetch it and add it to her duties of cooking and cleaning. He stood, stretched, and started for the packs, but stopped and picked up his cup and said, "I guess I'll be needin' this!" and sat it down on the rock he had used for his seat. He went to the packs and pulled out a heavy tan and brown clay jug and brought it to the fire. He pulled the cork, cradled the container on his elbow, and took a long swig direct from the jug.

"Wal, if'n you was gonna drink from the jug, what'chu want yore cup fer?" joshed Smitty as he reached for the jug.

Curly handed off the flagon and wiped his lips, "Just in case I wanted to be mannerly! Hehehe," he cackled. "Or if'n I get too drunk to lift the jug!" He laughed at his own remark and reached for a second go-round with the liquor.

But Smitty handed it off to the Professor, who gladly accepted it with one hand as he set down his plate with the other. He wiped the spout with his sleeve and lifted the vessel to his lips to chug-a-lug a more than ample share. He dropped the clay container from his lips and wiped them with his sleeve as he stretched to pass the jug back to Curly. Although the professor would never admit it, he had been a professor at a very old and well-established university in Virginia, but his drinking had ended that rather unceremoniously. His bitterness had driven him to the frontier and every time he thought of his experience, he tried to drown the memory in liquor.

After several rounds of passing the jug, it came up empty when Smitty accepted it from Curly. He shook it, scowled at Curly and rolled to the side to get to his feet and fetch another. He staggered to the packs, dug around, and came up with one and before taking a step back to the fire, he pulled the cork and took another long drink. He laughed as he stumbled back to his rock and handed off the container to Curly.

As he sat down, more like fell down, on his previously occupied seat he looked around and he saw Beatrice bending over to pick up the heavy dutch oven that had held the stew. As she started to rise, Smitty jumped up and swatted her rear. She was shocked and turned around with the dutch oven in one hand and the coffee pot in the other. Without hesitation, she threw the remaining hot, thick coffee at the man and it splattered all over his stunned face. Her roared and charged the woman who swung the big cast iron pot in defense, but it was too heavy to get a good swing and the man batted it aside. "I'll show you, you uppity negra!" he shouted as he slapped the woman, causing her to stagger to the side.

She dropped the heavy pot and looked around for any weapon, but before she could find anything, Smitty grabbed at her throat and pushed her to the ground. Her arms flailed to the side, then grabbed at his hair and face. Smitty roared and cursed and forced her arms to the ground as he straddled her at her waist.

Curly had joined the fray and grabbed her kicking feet and hollered at Smitty, "I got her feet! Get her Smitty!"

The professor was only temporarily stunned, then he rose, but a protest was not forthcoming. He walked to the side of the scrappers, looked down at the face of the enraged woman and laughed. He dropped to his knees beside her head and sat back on his heels and cackled like a mad man.

Caleb had stepped around behind the carcass of the bear and was peeling down the hide, when he realized there was a scuffle near the fire. He had seen the men fighting before and didn't think much of it, wanting to get the hide off the bear. But a sudden thought made him look and he realized they had his wife on the ground. Anger flared, and he frantically grabbed up the knife. Driven by his rage, a few long strides and he was beside the drunken trio. It was as if he was detached and watching himself, a black curtain drawing close beside him. He was deaf to the shouts and screams as he snatched a handful of Smitty's hair and brought the knife across his throat, almost decapitating the man. Caleb released Smitty, throwing his body aside like the piece of trash it was, and grabbed at a startled Curly. The big black man struck the wide-eyed Curly with his left fist and plunged the bloody knife into his throat, again and again.

The professor had fallen back and was trying to scramble to his feet, digging his toes into the dirt, but the heavy bulk of the angered Caleb drove him to the ground. With massive and thoroughly bloodied hands, Caleb jerked the professor's head back and broke his neck, almost ripping his head from his body. The monstrous black man didn't hear himself as he growled like a grizz and jumped to his feet, kicked the professor's body to its back and snatched the man's pistol from his belt. Caleb looked around to see Long Tom scrambling to his feet, looking toward his rifle that leaned against a tree. Caleb's nostrils flared, and his eyes grew wide as his lips parted in a snarl and he stepped toward the tall man, his teeth chomping like and angered beast of the woods.

Caleb had lost all reason and was driven by his blinding rage and blood lust. When he spotted Long Tom, Caleb snarled, and his squinted eyes did little to hide the fire that burned within. Though this man had been the most sympathetic of the group, all Caleb could see was another white man that did nothing to help his wife. When the others attempted their assault, Long Tom had turned away, doing nothing. Just the thought that this man could have stopped it and allowed it to continue, fired the flames of hatred in Caleb's heart.

Long Tom held one hand out before him, but quickly realized there would be no stopping the incensed and bloody man. The buckskinner dove for his rifle and cocked it as he rolled to his side, but he saw the flame from the pistol stab the stillness before him and he felt the impact of lead piercing his chest. He tried to suck wind, but another blow knocked him back, and another drove him to the ground. He looked to see the crazed figure of a man standing astraddle of him and glaring his hatred as he pulled the trigger and emptied the Dragoon into his chest.

Caleb heard the hammer click on an empty cylinder and he tossed the pistol aside. He breathed deep, smelling the black powder smoke, the stench of the bear and the coppery smell of blood. He looked to the pile of bodies beyond the fire and in sudden realization he ran to the side of his wife. He dropped to his knees, pushing off the body of Smitty and looked at the bloody face of Beatrice. For just a moment, he hoped the blood was that of the men he killed, but he knew it was hers. Smitty had slit her throat and her eyes stared at the grey sky overhead. Caleb dropped his face to hers and sobbed.

He stood and lifted his voice to the treetops and the roar started deep in his chest and his voice that normally sounded deep and mellow and pleasant, rose to a scream that echoed back from the far side of the valley and reverberated through the trees. Exhausted he dropped to all fours, his head hanging and tears wetting the ground beneath. His breathing was raspy, and he collapsed to his side, staring at the gently swaying treetops and he thought of the incongruity of it all. His wife lay dead, and in his mind her murder avenged, but he felt confusion, fear, anger, and more knowing his tomorrows were even more uncertain than at any time in his life.

Although Caleb had thought himself alone, less than a hundred yards away, two men had watched everything that happened and now turned to one another and grinned. "This man is a mighty warrior and he will join us!" declared Banni as he looked to Peenaquim. The leader of the Bloods nodded his head in agreement and motioned for the others to join them. They would go together to this camp. They would show this big black man that made them think of the bears that prowled these woods, how to get vengeance over the whites.

CHAPTER NINE
TOGWOTEE

THE TOWERING LIMESTONE ESCARPMENTS STOOD AS PALE sentinels, staring down the Wind River Valley and keeping watch over the distant plains. With the leader of the mountainous crags standing taller than the rest, it formed an imposing pillar that dwarfed the travelers moving slowly along the slope hugging game trail. Tate and his family traipsed on the south side of the twisting stream that snaked its way to freedom from the high mountains. Occasionally disappearing in the dense woods and shadows, the travelers relished the warmth when the sun found them in the open. The beginning of their trek was just below the basaltic ridge that was scarred with the slash of iron-rich red rock that tumbled from the pinnacle, and now they moved toward the notch that marked the crest of the Togwotee pass. Long used by raiding parties of northern Indians like the Blackfeet, Gros Ventre, and even the Shoshoni, it was the northern gateway to the southern plains and the territory of the Crow, Cheyenne, Sioux, and Arapaho. But these travelers were not of any of the tribes, though friendly to most. Tate Saint and

his family were making their way to the land of the Shoshoni
and his friend known as Knuckles or Big Fist.

Lobo and Indy were side by side, tongues lolling, and
maintained the ground-eating lope that kept them in the lead
of the entourage. Sean and Sadie followed close behind, with
Tate and Maggie leading the pack-horses. They were nearing
the headwaters of the Wind River and the trail on the
southern slope bent to the creek bottom and crossed to the
opposite hillside. Before leaving the trees, Sean reined up
and motioned for Sadie to stop, as he watched Lobo scout
the area below. When the wolf sat down at creek's edge and
turned to look back at the family, Sean gigged his horse
forward and they pulled up at the creek bank to give the
horses a breather. With a simple wave of the hand, Lobo and
Indy took off across the creek and up the hillside to scout the
trail ahead.

"Good choice, Son," commented Tate as he stepped down
from the saddle. And although she didn't need the help, he
offered a hand to his wife as she too took to the ground.

Maggie looked to Tate, "Are we going to lunch here?"

Tate lifted his eyes to the sun, looked back to his redhead,
"If you want. Or, we could ride a mite further."

Maggie looked around at the grassy creek bank, the clear
water of the mountain stream, and the shade of some nearby
aspen and answered, "Nah, here's fine. You wanna get a fire
going for coffee?" She looked to Sean, "How 'bout you seein'
if there's any Brookies in that stream and fetching us up
some for dinner?"

Sean smiled at his mom and trotted off to a wide bend in
the creek marked by a grassy undercut bank. He swung wide
of the curve, ensuring the sun was at his face and walked
slowly to the water's edge, dropping to all fours as he
approached. As he peeked over the bank, he saw several nice
sized trout and he bellied down to start his hand fishing. He

soon had four flopping Brook Trout on the grass but had to go downstream to the next undercut bank to get a couple more. Shortly, he had all six cleaned and on a forked stick as he carried them back to the fire and his waiting mother. She smiled as he approached and readily took the fish to roll in some corn meal and get started frying for their meal.

Since they stopped, Tate had been feeling a little antsy and once finished with his meal, he picked up his Sharps and looked to Maggie, "I'm goin' up on that rockpile an' have a looksee."

She nodded her understanding and began the clean-up so they could get back on the trail as soon as possible.

Tate walked through the tall grass, rifle cradled in his arm, continually scanning the far hillside. Where they stopped was down in the bottom of the valley and Tate liked the high promontories where he could see what was around. The hair on the back of his neck was prickling and he felt a little uncomfortable. He had just reached the rocks when Lobo came trotting up and Tate could tell there was something around the wolf didn't like. He dropped his hand to his side to touch the head of the wolf as he came near, and Lobo leaned against him, turning to look at the opposite side of the creek and let a low rumble come from deep in his chest. Tate knew that to be the wolf's warning of danger.

Tate dropped to one knee beside the boulders, pulled his scope from his belt and began to scan the area. Within moments he spotted movement and rested the scope on the spot. He whispered, "Two, no, four riders, Indians, but what are they?" He was talking to himself as much as to Lobo. "I think they might be Snake." As he watched, the four were slowly moving through the trees, apparently hunting, probably for elk or deer. They were moving toward the creek and would soon be within sight of the rest of his family. He cupped his hands to his mouth and mimicked the call of a blue jay to get Maggie's attention.

The familiar sound brought Maggie around and shading her eyes, she looked to Tate beside the massive rockpile. He quickly motioned for them to get behind cover, and that Indians were on the far mountainside. With a snap of her fingers and a whispered warning, Sean and Sadie came to their mother's side and all went to ground behind the willows. The horses were grazing in the clearing in the aspen grove and were not obvious, but not totally out of sight.

Tate watched and at the first chance, he went to a crouch and using what little cover was available, made it back to his family. He whispered, "There's four Indians, hunting, and I think they're Shoshoni, at least they look like it, but I think we'll soon know for sure." He motioned with his chin, "You two get your rifles but stay down. I'm goin' up there," another chin point, "and watch to see what they do. If they come too close or . . . I'll step up and confront 'em, but you stay down." At Maggie's nod of understanding, he trotted off, hunched low behind the willows, and found himself a sizable boulder to mount for his look-out.

Hunters in the Rockies know the deer and elk prefer to bed down in the thicker timber, but within sight of the grazing and watering area. The warriors were scattered through the dark woods, hunting, and came together at a point where the trees thinned, and the clearing of the valley bottom showed the willow-lined creek. It was also common to find the animals bedded down or grazing in the flats, staying near the water. Tate watched as the four conversed, often pointing to the stream, followed by spreading out in hopes of jumping some game from the willows, and approaching the stream slowly but watchfully.

Tate realized he was holding his breath and slowly let it escape as he stood, rifle cradled in his left arm and standing tall to reveal himself to the hunters. The warrior farthest upstream spotted him first and reined up suddenly, with a shouted "Ho!" to warn his companions. The warning was relayed until the hunter downstream from the others heard and turned back to his friends. Tate lifted his free hand, palm open and his arm extended as he looked at the warriors. Although well-versed in Comanche, Ute, and Arapaho, he could only use sign language with the Shoshoni. He didn't want to set his rifle down and awkwardly began to use sign to speak to the hunters. "I am a friend to the Shoshoni. I come to see a man called Big Fist. Is he with your village?"

One of the warriors gigged his horse forward and nodded, then spoke in English, "Big Fist is with our village. I am Chochoco, his son."

Tate grinned, "Then your mother is Pinaquanah. Big Fist is my friend, I am called Longbow."

Chochoco looked at the man on the boulder, "My father has spoken of you. I will take you to see him. Are these others," he waved his hand toward Maggie and the young-sters still crouching behind the willows, "with you?"

Tate grinned as he realized they had already been spotted before he stood and answered, "Yes, they are my family."

As Maggie and the youngsters rose and stepped forward, Chochoco noted the rifles in the hands of Maggie and Sean, then he looked at Sadie and asked, "These have rifles, where is yours?"

Sadie's hand held the scruff of Indy's neck and she looked down, "Don't need one, I have him."

The eyes of the Indian grew wide as he saw the black wolf step closer to Sadie and Chochoco looked from the wolf to the girl and back at the others.

"We will go now," directed Chochoco and turned to explain to his fellow-hunters.

.   .   .

As they entered the village, children and women followed alongside the visitors, most looking at Maggie and Sadie with their long red curls, an oddity in the mountains, others staring at the wolves that moved alongside the horses. Many had never seen a white woman, none had seen the red hair, and though most had seen wolves in the wild, none had seen them with people. Maggie listened to the comments and realized their language sounded similar to that of the Comanche. She had a certain knack for languages having learned Arapaho, Comanche, Ute and was beginning to understand Apache. This was her first time hearing the Shoshoni speak and she smiled as she listened to the similarities.

The village had over forty lodges and word spread rapidly about the visitors. By the time the small entourage reached the lodge of Big Fist and Pinaquanah, the old-timer was standing before their lodge, arms across his chest, grinning through his scraggly whiskers and watching.

He waddled toward the grulla that held his friend. Tate swung a leg over the rump of Shady as he quickly dismounted and greeted his old mentor and friend with a bear hug, each slapping the other on the back as they danced around in a circle, laughing at one another.

Tate pushed away and said, "You ol goat! You don't look a day older. Fatter maybe, but not older. This squaw life must be good for you!"

The older man rubbed his ample belly and grinned, "Ya got that right, pilgrim. But," lifting his eyes to the family, "who's these folks wit'chu?"

Tate stepped back, gave Maggie a hand down and when the youngsters were beside her, introduced, "Knuckles, this is my wife, Maggie, and my two youngsters, Sean and Sadie."

Knuckles stepped forward and extended his hand to Maggie, which she slapped aside as she gave the man a hug.

When she leaned back, "I feel like I've known you a long time. My man has talked about you often."

Knuckles dropped his head, pink showing on his neck and cheeks, "Awwww, go on now, he don't neither, less'n it's to talk bad 'bout me."

"Oh no, he wouldn't do that."

She was interrupted when Knuckles spied Lobo and dropped to his knees to greet the wolf, "Don't tell me this is Lobo?" looking at the big wolf and back to Tate. Lobo walked toward the man, sniffing, and with the memory that only a creature of the wild would have, accepted the embrace of the old man. "See thar, he 'members me!" But when Indy stepped forward, the old-timer rose to his feet and looked at Tate, "Another'n?"

Tate grinned, "I think he's one of Lobo's offspring. Lobo brought him to the cabin and he and Sadie kinda adopted each other."

"Just like her ol' man!" Knuckles stood and motioned for the family to follow him as he said over his shoulder, "Let's get you settled an' then we'll eat an' talk a spell. How's that?"

"That'll be just fine," answered Tate as he led their animals toward the lodge.

CHAPTER TEN
RAIDS

BANNI AND PEENAQUIM WATCHED THE CAMP BELOW AS CALEB busied himself with burying his wife. The big black man wore canvas britches but had stripped off his shirt when he was skinning the bear, and now on his knees he scratched at the rocky earth to dig the grave for his wife. He would often pause in his labor, arch his back and yell at the treetops, venting his anger, grief, and frustration. He carefully wrapped Beatrice's body in blankets, and gently lay her in the grave. Lifting his head to the sky, he spoke loudly, "Lawd, I don' know why you let this happen. We come this fah', got our freedom, an' you let her die!" he was shouting as he shook his fist at the heavens. "If that's the way you gonna be, I'm gonna kill me some mo' white men an' send 'em all to visit they's friend the devil!" His anger drove him into his past and he could only express his emotion in the vernacular of the field hand that labored in anger.

Caleb filled in the grave, covered it with massive rocks, and stood to look at the dead men around the camp. Every time he passed one, he either kicked the body or spat on it, almost unconsciously, showing his contempt. He began gathering the weapons, gear, and other supplies, to take stock of where he was and what he had. As he looked around, he sat down on a log, hung his head in his hands and silently sobbed. He didn't know if he heard or just sensed something, but when he lifted his head, he was surrounded by Indians, two holding rifles on him and the others with lances or bows held at the ready.

He looked from one to the other and as two stepped forward, Caleb slowly rose to his feet. He was an imposing figure, taller than any of the warriors and dark eyes staring but showing no fear. Broad sweaty shoulders, colossal arms, contrasted with the tapered torso over trousers that stretched tight across muscular legs. He clasped and unclasped his fists, tensing all his muscles. His cheeks moved as he ground his teeth and his upper lip lifted just a bit to show his readiness to fight. His chest heaved with each deep breath, but he did not move as he watched the men approach.

"I am Banni Sanglat and he," nodding his head to the man beside him, "is called Peenaquim. What are you called?"

Caleb was surprised to hear Indians speaking in English and he stuttered as he began, "Uh, uh, I am Caleb, what do you want?"

"We heard you say you wanted to kill men like these whites. We had come to kill these men, but we watched you kill them. You are a good warrior."

"They killed my woman."

"Do you want to kill more?"

Caleb looked around the circle of stoic Indians, then at the bodies of the men he killed. With another look at the stones over the grave of his wife, the anger stirred again, and he turned to Banni, "Yes. Ain't none of 'em treated me like a man and I ain't seen none that deserve to live."

Banni shook his head, letting a slight grin part his lips as he looked to Peenaquim, who also nodded. Turning back to Caleb he said, "You will be called Sik Kiáá yo, that means Black Bear." Banni looked around the camp and continued, "You have much goods and weapons. We will help you pack it and if you want to trade or give some of these," pointing to the other warriors, "some of the rifles or other things, that is up to you."

It took little time for Caleb to choose his rifle, knife, tomahawk, buckskins, moccasins, and other gear before motioning to the others to take whatever they wanted. He was well outfitted with a .54 caliber Hawken, a Colt Navy pistol, a Bowie knife and metal blade hawk, while the only buckskins that came close to fitting were those of the dirty Smitty. He chose to take them with him and clean them later, leaving his canvas britches on for the time being. While he had been assembling his gear, using one of the warbags of the traders to gather it up, he paid little attention to the warriors that scalped the four men and stripped and desecrated the bodies.

With the rifles from the buckskinners and the weapons taken from previous raids, most of the followers of Baani were armed with rifles or pistols. With the addition of Caleb, the raiding party now numbered ten, enough to take most any raiding or hunting party of Indians, or encampment of white trappers. The raiders had stayed near the Yellowstone River and were now in the Absaroka mountains just south of the river and upstream of the big bend where the Yellowstone bent back to the northeast. Well equipped with supplies after taking those of Caleb's camp, the group was only concerned about taking the lives and scalps of any they thought of as enemies. The lands of their adversaries lay to the south and they traveled several days before one of their men spotted a hunting party of Shoshoni, he reported to Baani and

Peenaquim and they began to immediately plan their attack.

Whenever an Indian hunting party went after meat, they would most often split up in groups of two or three hunters to hunt a wider area, unless they were after buffalo which required totally different hunting tactics. But in the mountains when the primary game was elk the men would need to move stealthily through the timber to find the elusive animals and the fewer hunters, the quieter they could move. With secondary targets being deer, big-horn sheep, and even bear, the same tactics were needed. Of a group of three, one would usually be a young novice hunter on his first hunt and his duties would be to hold the horses and help dress the game, all part of learning to be a successful hunter.

Baani and Peenaquim agreed to split their group into two and lay in wait for those parties. Choosing their locations and followers, the two leaders were soon at the head of their men, positioning themselves to take one or more of the smaller hunting groups. Baani had Caleb, Four Horns, Red Crow and his friend, Ugly Head. Peenaquim had the four men that followed him when they joined Baani.

The terrain was marked with rocky outcroppings surrounded by ponderosa, fir, and spruce. The timber covered the mountainside and from a distance was deceptive, appearing too thick to move through. But, as is so often true with forests of the Rockies, the pines reached for the sky and their lower trunks were devoid of branches, making it easy to pass through and see for considerable distances. The woods were interspersed with boulders and rocky upthrusts, and Baani chose one for himself and Caleb, then positioned Four Horns and the others across the clearing at about thirty yards. Between them lay a well-used game trail.

As they waited, Baani explained to Caleb, "These are Shoshoni, or Snake," he made the sign of the Shoshoni by holding his hand before his face, with the palm facing to the side, making a squiggly line down that resembled a snake. "They have always been the enemy of my people and we have raided each other's villages many times. This land was ours before they came and now we fight them just to hunt these hills. The Shoshoni killed my mother's family."

Caleb nodded his head in understanding as Baani motioned for silence, indicating the hunters were approaching along the game trail. Three Shoshoni warriors, one with a trade fusil, the others holding bows with nocked arrows, spread out about ten yards apart with the center man slightly ahead of the others. As they started through the notch between the boulder outcroppings, the raiders waited. Four Horns and his two struck first firing their newly gained rifles at the three, but they were unskilled with the white man's weapons and only scored a wounding blow to one of the hunters. The Shoshoni countered with the fusil and arrows, able to get off several arrows before Baani and Caleb struck from the rear.

Baani fired his rifle, striking one of the still standing hunters and dropping him as Caleb's shot struck the other just below the neck in the spine causing the man to fall on his face unmoving. The wounded hunters were trying to get to their feet when they were overwhelmed by Red Crow and Ugly Head when Crow struck his enemy with a tomahawk, splitting his skull and Ugly Head buried his knife to the hilt in the second man's chest. Baani stepped closer and the three warriors stood screaming their war cries just before dropping beside their victims to take their scalps.

Caleb, still by the rocks, sat staring at the carnage but was stirred from his trance by footfalls, and turned to see two Shoshoni warriors charging with hawks raised. He stepped from behind the rocks, used his rifle as a war club and caught the first man on the side of his head with the butt of the stock, lifting him from his feet with startled eyes as he fell to his back. The second man stopped and turned to face this black monster, but looked, mouth agape as he started stepping backwards, fear showing in his eyes. Caleb brought the barrel of the rifle down atop the staggering Shoshoni's head, cratering the man's skull, dropping him to the feet of Caleb. The man now known as Sik kiáá yo, or Black Bear, stepped back from the two, staring at the prostrate forms crumpled together.

Baani came to his side, "Aiiieee, you have taken two! Their scalps will decorate your lance!"

Caleb turned to look at Baani and back at the dead men. He muttered, "I don't want no scalps," and turned to go to the tethered horses. Killing the Indians was different than his revenge on the white buckskinners; this was killing for scalps, nothing more. Although Baani tried to explain the long-standing feud between the tribes, to just lie in wait and kill someone was different than exacting vengeance. A bitterness came to Caleb's mouth and he spat as he walked through the trees. The Blackfoot stared at this mysterious man, shaking his head as he bent to take the scalps of the Shoshoni.

When Peenaquim's group joined the others, his men told of taking two groups of three each. At the report all the warriors waved their trophies and shouted their war cries that echoed through the trees. Caleb sat quietly aboard the big black stallion he had claimed from the white men and watched the others in their triumph.

The following day, the raiders surprised four white men, trappers by their attire and gear, and swarmed over them before the men had a chance to defend themselves. All were killed, and their bodies mutilated. This was the first time Caleb had seen such atrocities, and he turned away from the carnage, remembering one of the men had fallen from his shot. He snarled and spat on the bodies as the Indians took their scalps and stripped them, taking their horses, and dividing the plunder among themselves. Now all the raiders were armed with rifles, although few could be considered capable with weapons they had never used, but the rifles were a symbol of their success and prowess, and were jealously guarded by each man. Caleb stood aloof from the rest, disturbed by their callous manner, but the Indians interpreted his solitude as one of pride and honor as he let the others have their will.

"So, yore thinkin' 'bout findin' them Nez Perce and doin' a little hoss tradin' are ya?" asked Knuckles as he leaned back on his woven willow back rest, stirring the coals of the fire with a long stick.

"Well, since we're up thisaway, I thought if we could find 'em without too much trouble, I'd like to see what they've got. The boy there," nodding his head toward Sean, "has him a mighty nice stud horse that came from them by way of a trader down south, and I'm thinkin' I'd kinda like to do a little horse breedin' and raise some o' them spotted ponies."

"They be good horses, that's certain sure. An' just 'bout any Injun or white man'd like to have himself one of 'em."

"You got any idea where they might be found? The Nez Perce, I mean?"

"Wal, they been known to pitch their summer camp atop that plateau south o' the Madison river, a time or two. At least that there's where I'd begin lookin'," drawled the old-timer.

Tate was watching the expression on the face of his whiskery friend and caught a sideways glance every so often and thought he might be leading up to something. On a hunch, he asked, "You interested in comin' along, you know, kinda like a guide or sumthin'?"

"Who, me? Why younker, I'm gittin' too old to go traipsin' roun' these hyar mountains!"

"Too old!? I never thought I'd see the day when you'd admit to being too old to do anything you wanted to do. Who you tryin' to fool? Can't be me, you know better!"

The old man grinned and cackled, showing his only two front teeth, one on top and one on the bottom, and he slapped the stick in Tate's direction, "I prob'ly oughter go with you to keep you from gittin' that fine family o' your'n lost and you losin' yore topknot! You pilgrims could git yor'-selves lost in your own barn!"

Pinaquanah and Maggie were seated across the fire from the men and were absorbed in their own conversation, but when they heard the raised voice of Knuckles, Maggie asked, "What are you two conspiring over there?"

Tate chuckled and answered, "Ah, I finally gave in and asked Knuckles to come along with us and he's thinkin' the only reason he needs to come is to keep us from getting lost!"

Pinaquanah snorted, "He gets lost going to the trees in the morning!"

Everyone laughed but Maggie added, "If he's coming, Pinaquanah needs to come too, so at least one of them can find their way home!"

"Well, for right now, we need to find our way to our bedrolls," suggested Tate. "If we're going, tomorrow would be a good day to start, don'tcha think Knuckles?"

"The sooner the better. I was startin' to grow roots! It'll be good to get back on the trail, especially since Sugar's comin' along!" he grinned at his wife who smiled coyly at the mischievous old-timer.

Sean and Sadie had already gone to the lodge for the

night and, with Lobo and Indy as pillows, they were sound asleep. Tate and Maggie were very quiet as they slipped into the lodge and went to their blankets. On the way back from the fire, they talked about the coming trek into the north country and about the possibility of getting more breeding stock for their planned horse herd. It had been a long-held dream of Tate's and was shared by Maggie. The appaloosa horses were well known for their strength, stamina, and were especially admired by the Indians for their extraordinary color patterns. But Tate liked those he had for their intelligence and spirit. Sean's stallion had been quick to learn and had shown himself faithful to his young master, traits that could not be taught, but were part of the breed.

As they crawled into their blankets, Maggie whispered, "It'll be good having them with us. Pinaquanah will help me learn the Shoshoni language and with a woman to talk to and learn from, I believe I will enjoy the trip even more."

"I thought you two'd get along. Although Knuckles acts and looks like he's older'n these hills, he's not. I think we figured one time he was only 'bout a dozen years older'n me, so that ain't old."

"I thought he was at least as old as my pa!"

"Nah, his grey hair and whiskers make him look it and he likes to play the part cuz Indians revere their elders, an' he soaks it up!"

Maggie giggled as she covered her face with the blankets and nudged Tate to cover up and get to sleep. If they were to leave in the morning, they needed all the rest they could get.

THE FIRST GREY light of morning was chasing the stars to their hiding places as Tate was returning to the lodge. His morning quiet time was spent in the trees beyond the stream and he heard a bit of a disturbance toward the middle of the camp as he neared their lodge. Knuckles stepped from behind a nearby teepee and motioned for Tate to join him.

Speaking softly, Tate asked, "What's the ruckus all about?"

"A huntin' party went out a few days ago, up north beyond the big lake o' the Yellowstone. There was thirteen of 'em, an' they got hit by a band o' Blackfeet an' only two of 'em made it back," explained Knuckles. "There'll be a bunch goin' back to get the bodies, so we can ride with 'em a spell, if'n ya' want." He looked to Tate for an answer.

Tate detected the hopeful tone of his friend's question and asked, "Do you think there's gonna be any chance o' runnin' into these Blackfeet?"

"Hard tellin', I don't know 'zackly where they was huntin' an' such, but if'n them Blackfeet follered them two fellers back, it might be a good thing to be with a bigger bunch o' our own people, leastways at first, I'ma thinkin'."

"Makes sense to me, but if you think we'll be gittin' into trouble, I ain't anxious to put my family in danger," explained Tate, looking at his friend for an answer.

"Wal, as long as they was to the east o' the big lake o' the Yellowstone, an' we be goin' to the west, should be alright. Where they're goin' is Crow country an' we be headin' toward the Gros Ventre and Nez Perce. Both them tribes are friendly with white men. They say they even got some missionaries amongst 'em."

Tate stepped back and looked at Knuckles, "You know, after I left you last time, I run into some missionaries that said they were goin' up to that country. By the sounds of things, I reckon they made it. Well, good for them." He was grinning as he shook his head, remembering the trip over Union Pass to the Rendezvous with the missionaries, Marcus Whitman and his wife, Narcissa, and Henry Spalding and his wife, Eliza. It had been quite a trip and it was after he parted company with the missionaries, that he returned and married White Fawn. He smiled at the memory.

The village chief, Shoots the Buffalo Running, or Washakie, asked his war chief, Weahwewa, Wolf Dog, to lead the band to retrieve the bodies. Twisted Hand, Owitze, or The Horse, and Po'have, were his sub-chiefs and each man led six warriors, one of those with Owitze was Chochoco, Knuckles' son.

The Shoshoni revered the dead and treated them with great respect. Referring to God as "Our Father" and some-times as the "Great Spirit," they believe that death is a pilgrimage to the land beyond the setting sun and the dead are reincarnated in another animal form. The dead would be carefully wrapped in skins and buried in caves or clefts in rocks together with their possessions for their journey. Whenever a chief died, his horses would also be sacrificed to join him on his journey. Weahwewa and his men were to retrieve the bodies and if possible, return with them to the village for burial, or if not, to bury them near the site of their death. It was a somber group, but one that was also prepared for any encounter with the Blackfeet.

Tate was relieved to be traveling with the larger group and Knuckles had been told the attack had taken place north east of the big lake of the Yellowstone and the survivors were certain they had not been followed. The first part of the day's travel took them west along the foothills and after a short mid-day rest, they turned to the northeast to follow a shallow creek until it came to a fork and the band stayed to the north keeping the creek on their right. As dusk began to fall, everyone was tired and willingly crossed the creek to the east side where there was more graze and a few juniper and piñon for some shade and cover. Several fires were kindled, and Maggie and Pinaquanah busied themselves together to prepare the meal for their group of six.

The lowering sun sent lances of pale orange to pierce the remaining clouds that bore brilliant skirts of blaze orange. The hillside caught the evening's glow as everyone gathered around their fires to enjoy their evening meal. Tate looked at Knuckles, "This ain't the way you sent me when we were in this country last time," motioning to the hillsides behind them.

"No, no, I didn't. But as I recollect, the village was camped over yonder below the plateau and you had to follow the Snake River outta there. But you did go over the Togwotee, didn'tchu?"

"Yeah, I did that."

"Wal, this hyar trail'll take us to the bottom o' the lake o' the Yellowstone, an' we'll part comp'ny with these fellas an' turn back to the west to find them Nez Perce. Course, that'll take us past that big geyser whut skeered you last time!" chuckled the old-timer, picking at his venison steak and pushing some beans around on his plate, remembering.

Tate chuckled at the remembrance and answered, "Yeah, you laughed at me that time too, you ol' galoot, you." Tate kicked at the man's moccasined foot, laughing.

It was good to travel through memories with friends. Living in the mountains and not being around people very often, those opportunities were rare and cherished by those of the wilderness. Maggie and Pinaquanah watched their men and Smells of Sugar looked to her new friend, Morning Sun, smiled, and said, "We will make our own memories."

CHAPTER TWELVE
WAGONS

ORDINARY MEN. MEN WITH CALLOUSED HANDS, BLISTERED feet, faces and arms sunburned and browned. Eyes that squinted at the bright great plains sun, leaving wrinkles that showed white against the leathery faces. None had buckskins, but they wore the uniform of civilization, canvas, cords, or wool britches, hanging from galluses over the Linsey Woolsey or gingham shirts and scuffed boots over hand-knit socks. Three had left their wives and children behind, one a widower, one with his wife, and the others with stories of lost loves and bitter experiences. They were greenhorns, pilgrims, easterners, without a lick of sense but all full of dreams and hopes. Farmers, stevedores, roustabouts, a bartender, store clerks, a stone mason, a liveryman, and a blacksmith made up the group, all from around the Westport, Missouri area. Each one desirous of a new start, and hopefully riches, in a new land, and willing to risk lives and savings in the chase.

Three wagons, loaded heavy, each behind a four-up hitch of mules that were slapped, derided, cussed, chided, and whipped to get this far without losing any cargo or life, trudged slowly on the chosen trail, whenever a trail could be found. They had traveled with a west-bound wagon train on the Oregon Trail until reaching the new Fort Clay, near the Platte River bridge, when their trails divided with the large train continuing on the Oregon Trail and the Owen group going north.

These men were following the hand-drawn map of George Owen's cousin, John Owen, who had been a sutler at Fort Hall and taken over the failed St. Mary's Mission and turned it into a trading fort named after himself. He had recently been appointed Indian Agent and had also discovered gold in the Bitterroot Valley. His letter to his cousin asked for help in rebuilding the wood stockade, offering the location of the gold discovery in exchange. Not one to get his hands dirty, he had kept the discovery a secret, choosing to let others do the hard work of mining while he collected a percentage and maintained his very lucrative trading post and position as Agent. The men of the wagons were to trade labor on the rebuilding of the fort for what promised to be rewarding claims. Believing they would be the first in the area, the men were anxious to get there and get started mining.

"So, George, vhat's this hydro . . . hydra . . . vhatever, stuff you got in that vagon?" George Owen, the one man with his wife, and Melvin Hyatt, the lone widower, were the organizers and leaders of the group of hopeful miners. They had been neighboring farmers and had a couple of very unprofitable years that made them susceptible to the promises of George's cousin. The man asking the question was Adolphe Peterson, the big swede that had been the blacksmith in his small farming community that was fading as fast as the drought.

"Adolphe, it's called hydraulic mining. I read about it being used out in California for their gold mining. It uses high pressured water to wash down the hillsides into sluices to capture the gold. A few men can do the work of hundreds in the same amount of time," answered George, picking up a stick to stir the coals beside the big coffee pot. They had stopped for the night and just enjoyed a big meal of fresh buffalo steak, skunk cabbage, and beans; and the entire crew was sitting near the fire, sipping their coffee. The conversation around the campfire was one of reassurance, the dreamers needing to be reminded of their goals. Most of the topics had been breached before, but after so long traveling, facing challenges and other difficulties, the men needed to be reassured the decisions they made were right, and the promises were still on the table.

"What if we want to go off on our own, do our own pannin' an' such," asked Jesse McCormick, the stone mason.

"The only thing we're obligated to do is to help my cousin on the rebuilding of his fort wall. He wants to replace the old wood with brick or adobe or stone, somethin' that'll last a mite longer."

"So, this cousin o' yours, how come is it he ain't goin' after all this gold?" asked Grant Marshall. The biggest of the group, Grant, had known hard work all his life, much of it spent as a stevedore on the docks at Independence, loading and unloading the many riverboats. Standing a bit over six feet, he seemed to be as wide as he was tall, barrel-chested, with massive arms, no neck, and a block-shaped head, his high ranging voice didn't fit the form.

"Wal, Grant, I don't know him very well, but if he's anything like his pa, and my pa said he was, he's plumb lazy, and the last thing he'd want is to get his hands dirty. He found the gold kinda accidental like. He went to the stream near where they camped, bellied down to get a drink and was staring right at a gold nugget the size of his little finger nail. It was just him and his wife on their way to the mission and he kept it to himself. He's one o' these planners and thinkers, always figgerin' out how to get somebody else to do the work while he counts his money."

Michael Mangini sat beside his son, Anthony, a young man of sixteen, and thought about his wife and daughters back in Westport and asked, "Are you certain this is gonna be enough of a strike to make it worthwhile? My family's wantin' to have a new home and it's gonna take money."

"Mike, like I said before, there's no guarantees, but with the equipment we got and bein' the first one's there, I'm bettin' we're all in for some rich times. But the way I look at it, if it's a total bust, that country is up for grabs and we could always start a new farm or somethin' like that. This is big country we're goin' to, and the only thing keepin' us from hittin' it big is our own selves."

"Hear, hear!" chimed in Thomas Specht, lifting his tin coffee cup as if in a toast. "Here's to the future! May it bring lots of gold and all th' other good things in life!" Thomas was one of two roustabouts that jumped ship from the riverboat at Westport. He told of stories of men bringing bales of beaver and other pelts and reaping high profits, all to spend it in the city and return to the mountains broke. When he spoke with George Owen about the possibility of gold, it was a hope to hang his hat on and he quickly signed on. Ever the optimist, he kept smiles on everyone's face with his tall tales, wild stories, and wishful thinking.

Michael Mangini asked, "What about Injuns? We only saw a few on the wagon train comin' acrost them flatlands, but I heard some folks talkin' back at Fort Laramie that there's been some fightin'. Especially where we're a goin'."

Owen stood, stretched and walked around the fire circle as he talked, "I had a chance to talk to General Harney when we were there an' asked him about it, the uprisin' I mean. He said that since the treaty of '51, things had been kinda quiet, until one o' the Mormons lost his milk cow and the Indians camped near the fort found it and killed it to eat. So, the former commander of the fort sent a wet-behind-the-ears lieutenant name o' Grattan to settle things with the Indians. Wal, seems that lieutenant got all uppity and threatened the chief an' one o' his men shot the chief in the back and things went downhill after that. Them Sioux killed all them soldier boys, twenty-nine of 'em, and then lit out for the hills. Let's see, that was in '54, then nigh unto a year later, the General, he decided to show them Sioux who's boss an' he hit their village o'er to the east, an' killed less'n a hundred of 'em, captured a bunch more, and then negotiated a peace treaty. So, here lately, things've been pretty peaceful. And of course, they put in that new fort down by the North Platte, Fort Clay, and put some soldier boys there."

George and Melvin Hyatt had been talking about the possibility of an attack by Indians, but neither man was worried. They did however, take stock of the weapons that everyone had and were pleased to learn all were armed. Some were better outfitted than others and most had replenished their arms and ammunition while at Fort Laramie. Melvin was the only one with a Sharps, while George and several others had Hawkens or percussion rifles. Two men had smooth bore shotguns, and one, Ebenezer Hardy, a former storekeeper, had a Colt revolving carbine shotgun and a Colt revolving ring lever rifle. Most also had handguns, like the Colt Paterson or Dragoon. All seemed to be capable with the weapons, and George and Melvin agreed they would present a suitable defense.

"So, what's our route now, and 'bout how long we got left 'fore we get there?" asked Hardy.

George smoothed a piece of ground with his foot and using a stick, began to describe their route, drawing a line as he spoke. "From here," marking an "x" on the ground, "we keep north by northwest along these mountains here," pointing behind him at the Big Horns, "until we get to the Yellowstone River. That'll be, oh, five to seven days, all things considered. Then my cousin said we follow the Yellowstone west until it takes a big swing to the south." He was drawing as he spoke, poking the ground at certain points for emphasis. "He said that'll take us 'bout ten days or so. Then we cross over and bear west for 'bout two weeks. We'll swing south o' some mountains 'long here," making a scratch above their route, "and have to cross o'er a couple ranges an' then we come to what he says is the most beautiful valley he ever did see. It's called the Bitterroot valley cuz' o' the river that flows in the bottom. He said it is green, grassy, beautiful, and goes on forever." He had lifted his head, and closed his eyes as he described the valley, imagining the scene in his head.

Melvin Hyatt poked Grant Marshall in the side with his elbow and chuckled as he nodded toward George, "That's the farmer in him talkin'."

Grant looked at Melvin with a sidelong glance and snarled, "I don't care 'bout no farmland. Long as that river's got gold in it, I'll be happy. But if it don't . . . "he shook his head and hit his palm with his fist, as if threatening harm to someone. Melvin scooted away and off the log, glancing from Grant to George and hoping the cousin had been right in about the gold that was waiting.

Two days after leaving the band of Shoshoni, Knuckles led the small party to a campsite that lay in the trees overlooking the shore of the big lake of the Yellowstone. Before choosing their stop for the night, they had crested a bald-topped rise that overlooked the entire valley. Knuckles, always the one to share his knowledge, pointed out the different lakes and the distant plateau where they hoped to find the Nez Perce. Behind them lay the higher mountains of the Absaroka Range and to the southwest stood a sizeable mountain that seemed to rise from a lake at its base. Their route, as Knuckles pointed out, would take them between the western shore of the big lake of the Yellowstone and another large lake to the west. He reminded Tate, "Yonder lies the big geyser that rolled you outta yore blankets. Hehehe, an' we'll prob'ly pass it tomorrow. Thataway your young'uns can see it. Our trail will bend round that smaller lake thar." He pointed out a hatchet-shaped lake with deep blue waters. When they arrived at their chosen camp-site, the crystalline blue sky bounced the last of the sunlight off the matching blue waters and slowly accepted the darkening blue that caught the random lances of deepening orange as the sun bid its adieux.

The twilight brought a restfulness to the camp as they gathered near the fire to dip the evening's fare into their plates. The group wasn't as tired as they were content. The beauty that surrounded them the entire day as they journeyed, the marvels of creation, the antics of the wildlife and the orchestration of the myriad of birds had given each one a contemplative mood. The smiles were common, the glassy stares contagious, and the comfort genuine. The conversation of the evening was in soft tones as the nighthawks cried into the darkness, to be answered by the ratcheting of the cicadas.

But the mellow mood was broken when Sadie cried out, "Eeewwww, what's that smell?" putting one hand to her nose to pinch it off from the odor. The breeze that had been blowing toward the lake, shifted its direction and now softly whispered through the pines to the south. While just north of the camp, several hot springs brought the clear waters from the depths to the surface, carrying the sulfurous minerals with it.

Tate and Knuckles chuckled, as the old-timer said, "That, young lady, is the smell of some hot springs up the bank a ways. They bubble up with some mighty purty water, but sometimes it stinks worse'n a polecat!"

"Can we see 'em tomorrow?" asked the curious Sadie, still holding her nose and sounding a bit strange, but she was always one for a new adventure.

"We'll be goin' right by 'em, and we'll be seein' some other wonders and water 'fore the day's o'er."

Sadie smiled and dropped her hand from her nose, and sat her plate aside, having lost her appetite with the smells.

She stood and stretched and went to her bedroll and with Indy at her side, she was asleep before the others had finished their meal. It had been a good day and the night's rest would be welcome.

THE TIMBER WAS tall and dense, but the well-used game trail wound its way through, always finding the easiest passage and only occasionally hindered by blow-downs. Knuckles led with Pinaquanah close behind, the youngsters were next in line, and Tate and Maggie, leading the packhorses, brought up the rear. Little sound was made as the horses trod lightly on the dense layer of pine needles and tundra carpet. Indy trotted beside Sadie and Lobo moved easily beside Tate.

A low rumble began deep in the earth and the ground beneath the riders trembled. Indy and Lobo froze in place, looking at the ground beneath them, feeling the movement as the trembling moved their paws. The horses began to nervously pace side to side, looking with wide eyes at the nearby trees that seemed to shake their limbs in warning. As the underground thunder increased, the children looked nervously back at their parents, Maggie looked fearfully to Tate, and when Tate's chuckle echoed the laughter of Knuckles, everyone else knew this was nothing to be alarmed about. Lobo looked up at Tate and turned back to look up the trail. Indy was looking back at his mentor and Sean was the first to speak. "Pa! Is that the geyser thing you talked about?"

"That's it, son. Nothin' to worry about. Just a big fountain of water in the valley up ahead. There'll be more so just settle your horse down and ride easy. You too, Sadie. Keep a tight rein." He looked to Maggie, "You too, babe. It might be a little scary for the horses till they get used to a few."

. . .

IT WAS mid-afternoon when they broke from the timber to a small meadow above the meandering river in the valley bottom. Knuckles stood in his stirrups to get the lay of the land and the others came up beside him. With hands shielding their eyes from the afternoon sun, everyone in the small party was taking in the broad vista of the open flats before them. They dropped back into their saddles just as the rumble started again. Knuckles spoke, "Looky yonder, there in that flat with all the alkali!"

As he pointed, the growl increased, and they watched the water boil from the ground. It spewed and sputtered, shot steam and water as the pillar of gurgling water rose higher and higher, showing white against the black timber beyond. The thunder was mixed with the hissing of steam and splashing of water and everyone seemed to ooh and ahhh in chorus as the plume danced before them. As it rose to a height taller than the surrounding trees, Maggie looked to Tate, smiled and pointed to the youngsters as they stood in their stirrups trying to see a little more. Sean and Sadie were looking at the geyser, back to one another, and to the geyser again. Although the water only danced for a few moments and slowly subsided, it seemed like the show had lasted much longer. When the last sputter hissed its goodbye, everyone relaxed in their seats and looked around to see the others' reactions.

The excitement of Maggie was mirrored in the eyes of Pinaquanah as she oooed and awwwed as much as the rest. Tate was surprised to learn this was the first time Pinaquanah had been here. Although her people had lived and hunted in this area for many years, she seldom left the village and this trip was an exciting adventure for her.

"Wal, looks like the show's over, folks. We'll foller this crick upstream a ways an' then we'll foller another'n up to the plateau yonder. If we make good time, we'll be able to soak these ol' bones in a hot springs 'fore we turn in for the night. It's one o' the few that ain't too hot to jump into. These other'ns would burn the hide plumb off'n a feller."

Maggie smiled at the thought of a hot springs soak. It had been some time since they enjoyed the hot springs in the San Luis valley below the Sangre de Cristo mountains. It had always been a treat to enjoy the springs and they usually met up with friends that came from the Utes to soak. The promise of the warm water and a restful night urged everyone on as Knuckles pointed his horse upstream.

As they rode, they passed a couple of lesser geysers, one that seemed to be constantly erupting, but others that spewed their waters intermittently. They stayed to the west of the meandering river in the valley bottom, keeping the basaltic rimrocked bluff off their left shoulder. The timber was scattered with several alkali flats holding the skeletal remains of long-dead trees that surrendered their leaves or needles to the mineral flats and boiling waters. The talus slopes that cascaded from the tall bluffs were occasionally marked with deep orange slashes that told of the origin of some of the mineral springs.

When they came to a confluence of a small crystal-clear stream and the wide, shallow river they rode beside they turned westward and followed the smaller creek to a notch in the bluff. As they entered the notch beside the water-course, a different crashing of waters told of a water-fall ahead. But just when they caught sight of the cascading waters, their trail turned up a slope that would take them to the top of the plateau.

The shoulder of the plateau held many ravines and gullies that would carry any runoff from cloudbursts and spring rains, but in this dry season, they were only hindrances to the trail. When Knuckles finally reined up at the edge of a cluster of aspen, he pointed just below the ridge and said, "Them hot springs is over yonder. We'll camp here tonight, an' we can walk o'er to them springs. Do y'all wanna soak or eat fust?"

Everyone looked at one another and Tate spoke for them all, "How 'bout we make camp, get a pot o' stew goin', then go soak while we wait?"

Everyone nodded their agreement and quickly set about their assigned tasks, anxiously looking forward to the refreshing dip in the hot springs. And they were not disappointed, as the springs were just the right temperature and the pool big enough for everyone. Knuckles said, "This is one o' the few that ain't too hot. Some o' them down yonder'd boil yore skin plumb off'aya. 'Course, only people are dumb 'nuff to do that. Animal's got better sense!"

"Speakin' of animals. Look over there!" declared Tate as he pointed to the alkali flats closer to the tree line. A big momma grizzly was leading her two cubs toward the stream that fed the larger river below. Whether going for a drink or to do a little fishing, she paid little attention to the group in the pool. At a distance of about three hundred yards, Tate wasn't too concerned, but slowly climbed from the pool, his union suit dripping, and went to the log where his Sharps rested. Everyone watched silently, but the bear was nonchalant as she waddled her way to the stream and disappeared in the willows.

"Uh, you all enjoy your dip. I'll just sit right here until she's gone."

And true to her nature, she was more concerned about her cubs than the intruders and the three soon wandered away into the thick black timber. Tate gave her a few minutes before he sat the rifle down and joined the others in the pool.

The brief reminder of the dangers of the wilderness brought a more temperate mood to the group and they returned to camp, anticipating a good meal and restful night. Maybe tomorrow, they would find the Nez Perce and make new friends and trade for some painted ponies.

CHAPTER FOURTEEN
NEZ PERCE

MOST OF THE LODGES OF THE NIMÍIPUU PEOPLE WERE THE same as those of other plains Indians; cured hides of buffalo, elk or deer stretched over the slender lodgepole pine uprights to form the conical tipi. A few of the lodges had tule mats as covering instead of hides, but all were of the same shape was not that different than so many others of the plains Indians. But the Nez Perce were a more peaceful people than most. The men wore buckskin tunics with long fringe at the sleeves and yokes and decoration of beads and quills over breech-cloths and fringed leggings. Beaded moccasins were worn by both men and women, with the women's being taller and reaching high up the calf. Their attire was not significantly different than other tribes, but they wore their hair differently. Where most other native peoples braided their long hair, the Nez Perce preferred to keep it straight, well brushed, and held back with beaded bands. A scalp lock decorated the top of the head and greased or waxed gathered bangs marked the forehead.

Two bands, the Alpowai and the Lam'tama, had gathered together for the summer hunts. The chief of the Alpowai,

Allalimya Takanin, or Wrapped in the Wind, was given the honor as chief of the combined bands while Tipiyelehne Ka Awpo, Eagle From the Light, usually guided the Lam'tama. The war leader and shaman was the respected Peopeo Kiskiok Hihih, or White Bird.

Their summer camp atop the Madison Plateau had been used by the Nimíipuu for many years. Their usual diet was mostly fish, but they supplemented their meat supply with elk, deer and buffalo taken during their summer hunts. The Nez Perce had been friendly with the whites, even though their homelands were becoming crowded with the many intruders. Several of the Nez Perce bands had signed the Treaty of Walla Walla, but these that camped on the plateau had chosen to maintain their way of living, independent from the whites.

THE CAMP of the Nez Perce was nestled in a wide caldera with thick grass and two spring fed streams. Low hills and bluffs rose on all sides with a wide saddle holding the trail that Knuckles followed into the hollow. He reined up and waited for Tate to come alongside as he looked at the village beyond. "Looks to me like about seventy or eighty lodges. An' that's a purty good sized bunch yonder," nodding his head to the west of the village. A large herd of horses was contentedly grazing in the deep grass and Tate guessed there to be well over a hundred head of horses, perhaps nearer two hundred.

The men sat their mounts, as did Maggie and the youngsters behind them, and watched as a group of five Indians cantered their horses toward them. Each man held a lance or a war club, three had war shields, but the leader gigged his horse nearer the visitors and spoke in sign. "Who are you and why are you here?"

"I am Big Fist, this is Longbow," motioning to Tate, "and we have come to trade with the Nimíipuu."

The warriors looked past the men to see the women and children, slowly nodded their heads, understanding no man comes to make war while traveling with women and children. They motioned for the group to follow as they swung their mounts around to lead the visitors back to the village. The group, with warriors before and behind them, entered the village amidst a crowd of women and children that stepped back with mothers shielding their youngsters from the wolves that trotted before the intruders. Most had never seen wolves this close and to see them in the company of white men alarmed the villagers. The people believed in Weyekins, or spirits that linked the people to the invisible world of power and protection, and these spirits were sometimes thought of as animal tokens. But never had they seen the spirits as live creatures that accompanied their beings.

As they neared a central clearing, they spotted a fire ring with several seated warriors. The men, obviously the leaders and elders, stood to observe the visitors. The leader of the accompanying warriors spoke, "They say they have come to trade."

An impressive figure, a blanket draped over one shoulder, his fringed and beaded tunic showing and his hair draping over his shoulders and his entire face painted red, glared at the intruders, and greeted them in English. "I am Allalimya Takanin, or Wrapped in the Wind, the leader of the Alpowai, and this village. You have come to trade?"

Knuckles looked to Tate, giving him a nod to answer, and Tate stepped down from his mount to address the man. "Yes, we have heard of the fine horses of the Nez Perce. We have two and would like to trade for more. I am Longbow," and nodding toward Knuckles, "and this is Big Fist. I have trade goods," he motioned to the packhorses, "and would like to trade."

The chief looked from Tate to Knuckles and then to the women and youngsters, "This man is with the Shoshoni!" he spat the words in disgust, for the Shoshoni were long-time enemies of the Nez Perce, although there had been few conflicts between the tribes.

Tate looked from the chief to Knuckles, chuckled and answered, "We are friends with many different peoples. His woman is of the Shoshoni, but he is of his own tribe. We have traveled among the Arapaho, the Crow, the Comanche, the Kiowa, the Osage, and others. We are not the enemy of the noble Nez Perce; we are your friends. Have not the Nez Perce signed papers of peace with the white man? Will you trade with us?"

Wrapped in the Wind looked from Tate to the others, then around his circle of leaders who appeared to speak with their eyes, and he answered Tate, "We will trade. But first, we will show you your lodge and then we will eat." With a wave of his hand, he dismissed the visitors. A woman came to Tate's side and motioned for him and the others to follow as she led them to a large tipi at the edge of the encampment. She motioned for them to tether their horses in the nearby trees where there was ample grass and a nearby trickle of a stream, and softly spoke, "I am Whispering Dove, I will return for you." She padded quietly away without looking back.

THE LEADERS and elders were seated in a circle around the fire and Tate and company were directed to seat themselves on blankets to the left of the chief and his close subordinates. They were near enough for conversation with the leaders and all were served by several women that distributed wooden platters to them. They expected the usual fare of venison and vegetables but were surprised when their platters held a variety of smoked fish and some vegetables and a blend of berries. As the women brought the platters, they would sneak looks at the redhead and the girl, obviously curious about the unusual color of their hair. But Maggie just smiled and accepted her platter without speaking.

Whispering Dove knelt before them and explained as she pointed to the different items. "These are *ci'mey* or whitefish," and as she pointed, "*pi'ckatyo*, brook trout, *wawa'lam*, cutthroat trout. This is *qém 'es*, sweet camas, and," pointing to the berries, "*cemi'tk*, elderberries and *ti'ms*, chokecherries." Again, she stood and padded quietly away.

Maggie looked to her man, "This is really quite good. The fish are smoked and very tasty."

"Ummhummm," answered Tate, busily eating the unusual fare. Each one held their platter near their chin and used their fingers to gather the tidbits. It was the usual manner of the wilderness, but strange to the youngsters who had always used tableware and were often reprimanded for using their fingers. Sean was enjoying himself as Sadie fussed and struggled but shared her food with Indy. Lobo lay quietly beside Tate with his eyes constantly moving and missing nothing.

When the women retrieved all the platters and the meal was over, Wrapped in the Wind turned to face Tate, "You are different than other white men. You have wolves for friends and you speak of people we do not know. You said you were a friend of many peoples, one I do not know. Osage, who are these people and where?"

Tate knew this man, the leader of these Nez Perce, was speaking to learn more of the man before him and to add to his own knowledge. Among the native peoples as with others, knowledge is power, and for this man whose travels were limited, his quest was to gain knowledge from those that visited his village. Tate scooted around to face the leader, "The Osage are a people who live beyond the great plains. To get to their land, one would have to travel the entire season of hunting. They are a peaceful people and the men grow very tall, taller than anyone here, including me. They live in the land of the whites and are at peace with them and have taken many of the ways of the white man as their own."

"Are there others like them?"

"There are many. The Cherokee, the Iriquois, the Mandan, the Pottawatomie, and others."

"Some of these I know." He looked long at Tate and asked, "You said your name is Longbow, but I see no bow, how is this."

"I do use a bow and it is called a longbow." He motioned to one of the nearby warriors who sat by his lodge with his quiver and bow nearby, "Your warriors have a bow of this length," he held his hands out at about the length of a usual bow, "but my bow is as long as I can reach." He extended his arms to his sides, hands outstretched. "Your warriors can easily shoot from horseback, but I cannot. But, I can shoot an arrow twice as far and still bring down a large animal."

The expression on the face of Wind was one of doubt and the two men near him spoke to one another, laughing at the claim of this white man. Tate dropped his eyes and grinned then continued, "My son, Bear Chaser, also does well with his bow."

"And your woman, how is she called?"

"She is Morning Sky and my girl is called Dancing Owl."

"Where is your village?"

"Our home is south of the Arapaho and the Crow."

Wind turned, gesturing to the men beside him, "This is Tipiyelehne Ka Awpo, Eagle From the Light, and our war leader and shaman is Peopeo Kiskiok Hihih, or White Bird.

We will do our trade after first light." He stood, wrapping his blanket about him and went to his lodge. The other leaders and elders also stood and started away.

Tate looked to Knuckles and his family and said, "I reckon that's our invitation to go back to our lodge and turn in for the night." He stood, gave Maggie a hand and helped her to her feet, and followed Knuckles back to the lodge.

MAGGIE AND PINAQUANAH CHOSE TO STAY NEAR THE LODGE and spend time with Whispering Dove, to learn of the ways of the Nez Perce. Lobo and Indy stayed with Sean and Sadie and the two joined three other youngsters on a trek through the nearby trees. With all the trade goods loaded onto one packhorse, Tate led the animal as he walked beside Knuckles to the central clearing to begin their talks.

Tate arranged the goods on the blanket before seating himself on the nearby log to await White Bird's examination of the items. There were the usual strings of trade beads, small metal bells, mirrors, hand knives, tomahawks, a small stack of blankets, some vermillion and Verdi Gris, one percussion cap long rifle and a Hawken, both taken from the Crow in their last conflict. Tate watched White Bird looking through the goods, noticing the man's occasional glances toward the rifles, but trying to ignore the weapons, believing too much interest would put him at a disadvantage in the trade.

White Bird looked at Tate, "You want to trade for horses?"

"Yeah, I have a good stallion, and was hopin' to get some nice mares, dependin' on what you have."

White Bird motioned to a nearby warrior, who appeared to be waiting, and at the signal from the Shaman, trotted off toward the horse herd. White Bird continued to examine the goods, motioned for a woman to look at the blankets, and picked up a tomahawk to test its heft.

When Tate saw the woman, he went to the pack, and brought out a cast iron dutch oven and sat it beside the blankets. The woman's eyes grew large as she looked at the treasured prize. Tate didn't know, but some of the women in the village had metal pots and even frying pans, but none had one like this which had been seen but never owned. Tate motioned to the pot and said, "My woman cooks biscuits and bread in one like that. Mmmmm," he rubbed his belly and licked his lips as he spoke. She smiled at him, looked at her man, and pointed, saying something in their language and walked away. Tate hadn't understood the words, but he certainly understood what she told her man, and he grinned.

Tate heard the hoofbeats of several horses and looked up to see the young man previously sent away was now leading three and another young man leading three more. They stopped across the fire ring from the traders and waited. White Bird motioned to Tate to look at the horses and Tate and Knuckles rose, walked to the animals to appraise them. Both men took their time walking around each horse, lifting their feet, examining the legs, looking at the teeth to determine their age, looking at their eyes to see the manner of each one, and going on to the next one to repeat his examination.

One mare was leopard spotted, with a white coat sprinkled with black spots of varying size, giving the animal the spotted look over her entire body. Tate liked the look, size, and age of this one above the others and the soft eye showed a gentle and intelligent spirit. The animal stood stock still through the examination.

Another mare, with a blanket of spots on her rear and with black mane and tail over its bay coloring, also had a soft eye, big rump and well-muscled chest, also stood quiet as she was examined. But the third mare, had wide eyes, appeared scared, but was well-built, had shown a jittery manner that moved away from any touch. This one Tate passed on by, looking to the next.

There were two others that Tate liked, both with the blanket of spots on their rear, but one more leggy than the other and showed it would be an animal with speed. The other was the smallest of the group but was gentle and quiet as well as with great conformation. He looked at the group one last time and returned to the log by the blanket with the trade goods.

Eagle From the Light had joined White Bird and was also looking at the variety of goods arrayed on the blanket. White Bird picked up the Hawken, lifted it to his shoulder and aimed down the barrel, then with a close examination of the weapon, he sat it back on the blanket.

Tate began, "There's four of those," nodding to the horses held by the young men, "that should do for me. What would you need for those?"

By the time the dickering was done, Tate had given both rifles, the dutch oven, several strings of beads, blankets, mirrors, and two twenty-dollar gold pieces for the four horses. But he was satisfied with the trade, knowing the mares would be the foundation of a good horse herd, even though it would be a task getting all the additional animals back to their cabin in the Wind River mountains.

IT WAS QUITE a caravan that left the village of the Nez Perce as the first swords of light pierced the darkness. Knuckles, Pinaquanah, Sean and Sadie each led an appaloosa mare, Sadie with the smaller easy going one that took to the girl at first sight and of course had been claimed by the girl. Tate and Maggie led the packhorses and Lobo and Indy were scouting the trail ahead. They had taken a couple of days to get the new horses comfortable with the presence of wolves, but with the people always nearby when the wolves were present, they adapted quickly. Knuckles chose a different route back to the camp of the Shoshoni and the procession was southbound across the Madison plateau.

"We'll be goin' toward that thar lake below them Tetons. Some'r callin' it the Teton lake, others just callin' it the Snake River lake. It ain't near as big as the one of the Yellowstone, but we should make it, oh, 'bout dark, mebbe before," explained Knuckles. The group had stopped for a mid-day breather for the horses and a time for some coffee and eats. Their travel had been easy as they moved across the flat plateau, but they knew the more difficult part of the day's trek lay before them.

The journey was enjoyable as Maggie and Tate made it a learning experience for the youngsters. At the sighting of every animal or unique plant, they would ask one or the other to name the object or creature. Tate was surprised as they not only answered, they would usually add something, maybe a description of the plant, its usefulness, or perhaps the call of the forest being. When Tate pointed to the sky at a circling bird, he asked Sean, "What kind of eagle is that?"

Sean looked at the bird and back to his pa, "That ain't no eagle, Pa, that's an Osprey! Eagles don't have that white belly and their calls are more like," and he mimicked the peeps of the Osprey, "and the eagle makes more of a chirp sound, like," and he cupped his hands to his mouth and gave a good imitation of the eagle's chirps.

Tate looked at Maggie, "Did you show him how to do that?"

She grinned at her man, "No, he just listens and tries to call the birds to him. He's really quite good."

Tate looked around and in a slight swale below them, he pointed, "Alright, Sadie, what's that long-legged thing down yonder, there by that little pond."

"Oh Pa, that's a moose, a mama and her calf, ever'body knows that!"

"So, what kind of sound does it make?"

Sadie looked to her brother and motioned for him to make the sound, she had heard him do it before back at their cabin by the lake. Sean cupped his hands and pinched his nose and let loose with an ooooohaaahhhhhuh sound that surprised Tate, especially when the moose lifted her head to look in their direction.

Tate shook his head at the boy and looked to Maggie, "That boy's good!"

Maggie showed a broad grin and nodded her head. "He can do a lot of sounds, that's what he does when he goes wanderin' in the woods."

The lessons continued as they traveled, with adults and youngsters learning from one another. By late afternoon, Knuckles led them off the plateau to a grassy bottomed wide valley with two creeks converging. The trail had followed the edge of the timber across a bald flat before cutting back through a point of pines that took them to the valley below. Tate asked Knuckles, "Is that the Snake?"

Knuckles grinned, "Yup! You just might make a mountain man after all, pilgrim. That there," pointing to the smaller meandering creek that showed through the trees, "is Polecat crick and the bigger'n is the Snake."

Maggie laughed at the men, "Who named these things? Polecat? Snake? We even crossed over the Crazy Woman."

Maggie looked to Pinaquanah, "Had to be some men that had too much to drink!"

Knuckles answered, "Wal, don't know who named 'em all. First ones that I know of whut came through hyar was John Colter, Jim Bridger, an' Jedediah Smith. But them mountains," he pointed over his right shoulder to the craggy granite peaks, "was named by some Frenchies. They's called the Tetons!" He lowered his voice and spoke to Tate, "I'll leave it up to you to tell her what that means!"

He led the group closer to the stream and called over his shoulder, "We'll cross o'er hyar, 'fore the two get together." He gigged his mount forward and led the way across the shallow stream to a wide sandbar and on into and across the wider river. Neither were a challenge to the experienced travelers and the grassy flat on the other side beckoned, giving the horses ample motivation to willingly make the crossing.

Their chosen site was bounded on three sides with timber and on the fourth by the river, but the men fashioned hobbles for all the horses to give them the freedom to graze and roam. The camp chores were readily undertaken, and all were soon seated around the fire for the evening meal. The sun appeared to be snagged on the jagged peaks and cast its brilliance in one last gesture to the day, before dropping behind the mountains and giving its light to the silhouettes of the peaks. It had been a good day of travel, and as the conversation ebbed, everyone soon turned in for the night.

As Tate lay with hands clasped behind his head, he looked at the stars that were peeking from the deepening darkness. Maggie turned on her side and looked at her man. "I've been thinking."

Tate turned to face his woman, smiled, "Oh?" and waited.

"Ummhumm, when we were quizzing the kids, I couldn't help but think about their future. I mean, for Sean, here in the woods following your example, he's beginning to show the kind of man he's going to be, what with the reading he does and all. He's already read every book we have, and always wanting more. He's been through the Bible at least once, maybe more. And he loves the wilderness and he idolizes his dad."

Tate grinned and asked, "And what's wrong with that?"

"Nothing, I think it's great. Like I said, he's growing into the image of his father. But . . . I'm thinking of Sadie."

Tate's forehead wrinkled as he looked, wondering, at his redhead. "What about Sadie?"

"Oh, I don't know, I guess I'm just wondering about what kind of life this is going to be for her. It's different with me, I grew up in Ireland and back east, had a good education, met a lot of people. But, she won't have that, and with all these problems with the Indians . . . " she let the thought dangle between them.

Tate breathed deep, looked at his wife, and pondered her words. He had always assumed his family would be with him forever, the children would grow up in the mountains and all, but, he also realized his thoughts were the thoughts of a man and what Maggie said would bear some consideration. "I see what you mean. We came north because of the problems with the Ute and Apache, then we run right into more problems with the Crow and now the Blackfeet. I've thought about it, but I was just thinking of the safety of you and the young'uns, but . . . I don't know. We're going to have to do some thinkin' and a whole lot of prayin', I reckon."

Maggie smiled, moved closer to her man, and kissed him, holding his cheeks in her hands, and said, "That's why I love you so much. You're always thinking about others and wanting to do the right thing. I couldn't ask for a better man. Thank you, sweetheart." She kissed him again and he wrapped his arms around her and drew her close. After all, it was a little chilly in the mountains after dark.

JOHN OWEN HAD COPIED HIS MAP FROM ONE FOUND AT ST.
Mary's Mission that was said to have been drawn by Jedediah
Smith, an early explorer of the area. It was that copy that lay
in the lap of George Owen as he sat on the flat boulder overlooking the flat plains to the north. With his finger on the
map, he followed the Clark's Fork to its confluence with the
Yellowstone. His cousin said the easiest way to distinguish
between the rivers was that all those he would cross would
be running to the north, but the Yellowstone, at least where
they would meet up with it, flowed from the west directly
east. George lifted his eyes, shielded them with his hand and
stared into the distance at what appeared to be a long line of
green stretching across the northern horizon. Using his brass
scope, he easily recognized the river as their goal.

It had been six days since their party had left the rest of
the wagons at Fort Casper. According to his calculations and
the word from his cousin, they were right on schedule.
Another day would get them to the Yellowstone and they
would turn west. He looked below at the three wagons,

arranged like a horseshoe with the Clark's Fork on the open end. The animals had been tethered on the grass nearby and grazed contentedly. The cookfire was going and the fading light was showing the color of end of day. George grinned to himself as he started to stand to return to the camp. But off to his left, at the edge of the trees, he saw movement. He slowly slid to his belly and brought up his scope, the movement showed but an instant, and he was certain it was a horse with rider. But they were gone into the dark timber leaving him to wonder as to the identity of the rider. He waited, keeping his eyes on the tree-line, but nothing else moved. Whatever, or whoever it was, had disappeared in the darkening woods.

George walked up to the fire where everyone was gathered. His wife had gladly taken the job of cooking, although she occasionally sat back and let the men try to show their independence but was always coerced into taking the job back. The big pot of stew wafted its aromas on the evening breeze and the men formed a line to get their plates filled. Anthony Mangini, the youngest of the group, had assumed the task of pouring the coffee from the big enameled pot.

As everyone found a seat or at least something to lean on, George spoke up, "Like I figgered, this here's the Clark's Fork of the Yellowstone. Looks like we got a couple other'ns to cross 'fore we get to the Yellowstone, an' if ever'thing goes alright, we should be campin' on the banks o' the Yellowstone 'bout this time tomorrow."

His announcement met with nods and mumbles of approval, but all were busy at their meal and reserved any questions or comments. "There's somethin' else." His tone caught each man's attention and they paused in their eating to listen. "I saw a rider, just a glimpse 'fore he went into the trees. Don't know if it was a white man or an Indian. I'm thinkin' it was an Indian, cuz a white man would prob'ly come down to get some supper. But he was gone 'fore I could make sure."

"Wal, them other Injuns we saw was friendly, maybe that'n is too," suggested Jesse McCormick, looking around at the others for their opinions.

"Yeah, the ones we met, what, three days ago, they just wanted to do some tradin' and such, weren't them Crows?" asked Grant Marshall.

"Yeah, they were Crow, but accordin' to what that general back at Fort Laramie said, the closer we get to the Yellowstone, the closer we get to Blackfoot country. I think we're outta the Crow territory. And the general said the Blackfoot ain't none too friendly with anyone," answered George.

"Ain't no Injuns, don't matter what kind, are gonna keep me outta the gold country! We'll just need to keep our eyes open an' our weapons ready!" declared Grant.

The others nodded their heads, several answering with a "Yeah!" or a "That's right!" but each man returned his focus to his food and coffee. There was little said for a while until all were finished with the clean-up and were seated around the fire. The mesmerizing dance of flames brought the usual night-time stare at the fire with glassy eyes that told of thoughts of distant places and times.

The time of solitude in the midst of a crowd was interrupted by Melvin Hyatt, "I agree with Grant, nothin's gonna keep me from the gold, but are we doin' enough? I mean, maybe we outta think about guards an' scouts, an' such. I'm thinkin' we'd be wise to be a little better prepared, don'tcha think?" He looked around the circle at the others, waiting for any response.

George thought a moment and opined, "Maybe Mel's right, we can't be too careful. I'd rather lose a little sleep than lose my hair."

"So, vhat you tink ve ought to do then, George?" asked Adolphe Petersen, the big Swede.

George stared into the fire, thinking, "To start with, how 'bout we double the guard. Two men at a time, and each man stands guard for a four-hour shift, shifts to change each night. That's six men per night, so everyone'd get a full night's sleep ever other night."

"But, that's only twelve men, an' there's thirteen of us, who you leavin' out?" asked Thomas Specht, always the joke-ster and curious one.

"I figger my wife could use all the help she can, so I think Anthony there could be her permanent helper, an what with havin' to be up so early an' all, and havin' to go out huntin' to get us fresh meat, that'd be his fair share. Course if there's one o' you fella's that'd like washin' pots an' pans better . . . " he grinned as he looked around the circle. No one volunteered to trade places with Anthony.

"Then I'm thinkin' we should have two scouts, out front and behind, and one each out to the flanks. That way if there's trouble, there'd be others to help. That leaves two per wagon, one watchin' an' one drivin'. So, what does ever'one think?" added George.

Ebenezer Hardy asked, "Those jobs rotated too?"

"Ummhumm, every day each one does somethin' differ-ent. That way we'd always have fresh eyes on the lookout."

Nodding heads showed their agreement, and all were affable on the drawing of straws, or in this case willow twigs, for the assigning of jobs for the night and the following day. Not everyone was happy, but all accepted the drawing as the only fair way of dividing the tasks, and those that were not on first-watch, went to their bedrolls to get what rest they could before their turn on guard.

. . .

THE DAY STARTED WELL ENOUGH, but as they crossed the Clark's Fork to begin their day's journey, the second wagon slipped coming from the water, slid back against a large rock and busted a rear wheel. They had to drag the wagon from water's edge and get it on the flat bank before beginning their repairs. Their foresight had provided a spare wheel and with the extra tongue as a lever, they soon had the broken wheel replaced. But patience and tolerance were in short supply among the wet, muddy travelers, and angers flared between Jesse McCormick and Thomas Specht. Jesse had been a stone mason and Specht a roustabout so both men were well-muscled and when they tied into each other, fists flew, blood splattered, and both were wetter and dirtier than when they started. It took the big man, Grant Marshall, to pull the two apart and as he held each man by his shirt collar, he hollered, "That's 'nuff!" They twisted and kicked in his grip, but he dragged both men to water's edge and with little effort threw them into the deeper water in the eddy. When they came up sputtering and fighting for air, they were less concerned about the other than about getting to the bank. Grant stood on the grassy bank, arms crossed on his chest, and watched as they climbed out, glaring at each other. Grant asked, "Are you done? If not, how 'bout another dip?"

The two grapplers looked at one another, up to the big referee, and both nodded and mumbled, "We're done."

"Good. When I said no one's keepin' me from the gold, that includes you!" declared Grant as he turned and stomped to the first wagon, climbed aboard, and slapped reins to the mules. Fortunately, the two fighters were on different wagons, but both had to run to catch up to their rides. McCormick was riding with Michael Mangini and Specht with Schmidt. Their job was to ride with rifles ready and eyes on the watch, but first they had to get dried off and cleaned up, which was difficult sitting on the wagon seat.

They crossed three smaller creeks before they pulled up to give the animals a breather and for the mid-day meal of left-over corn-bread, meat, plus a handful of fresh huckle-berries. Adolphe Petersen had been riding left flank and when he stepped down from the saddle to get his food, he looked to George Owen and asked, "Dat rider you saw, paint horse?"

George nodded, "You see him?"

"Ya, I tink so. He vas Indian, sure 'nuff. Dere vas two!"

"Were they watching us?"

"Ya, dey vas. Dey knew I saw dem, did notting."

George looked to Melvin and asked, "Wonder what they were doing. Lookin' us over, ya think?"

"Could be, but if there's only two of 'em, we don't have anything to worry about," answered Melvin.

"My guess is where there's two, there's gonna be more. We need to let the others know."

"They'll all be here in a short while to get their eats. We can tell 'em then. But I don't know what else we can do. Just be wary I guess."

George looked to his friend and nodded, wondering just what awaited them in the next few days and miles. They had been lucky this far and not had any real run-ins with hostiles, but it's not like they expected to make it all the way without some kind of conflict. He quietly reassured himself as he looked around the group that these men were prepared and capable and they could readily defend themselves against any attack. He just wasn't too sure because they had not been tested and no one is any good until proven.

CHAPTER SEVENTEEN
AMBUSH

THE AFTERNOON PULL WAS PROVING TO BE MORE DIFFICULT than anticipated. The many ravines, gullies, dry creek beds, all required the up and down pull to get to the flats above. Once atop the wider plateaus, it was easy to see there were many more obstacles of a similar nature before them. Each time the mules topped out on the flats, they had to be given a few minutes to blow and catch their wind. The long-eared breed had a reputation of stubbornness, but given sufficient rest and toleration, they proved their worth. The men were also growing weary, as they were often needed to push the wagons up the sandy slopes or at least utilize the blocks to keep them from rolling back down if the mules paused or weakened in the pull. Sweat painted streaks through the dust covered faces of the men and shirts were wet through. Some had removed the shirts entirely but were forced to put them back on when the sun was unrelenting with its blistering flames.

George Owen and Ebenezer Hardy sat on their mounts at the edge of a long bluff that overlooked the valley of the Yellowstone. George leaned forward with one arm on the saddle horn, removed his hat and wiped the sweat from his forehead. He let the slight breeze cool his face and wet hair as he scanned the edge of the bluff searching for an access to the river bottom. Ebenezer stood in his stirrups, pointed, "Look yonder, where that long draw breaks the bluff. Mebbe we could follow it down to the bottom. Looks like there ain't no water in it, and we could use the creek bed."

George also stood in his stirrups, replaced his hat to shade his eyes, and looked at the long ravine. It was wider than most, although this entire slope was scarred with run-off ravines carved when winter snows sent the waters in search of the river bottom. He reasoned this whole flat would be easy traveling except for the many gullies. The flat-top plateaus held nothing but bunch grass and cacti with only a smattering of juniper and cedar, the only green to be seen was beside the rivers or feeder creeks. He dropped back into his saddle, "Yeah, looks like a possibility. The river bottom sure looks easier, course we'll have to cross over. But if we make it alright, there's plenty of green for the mules and easy goin' for a long stretch. Maybe we can make up some o' that lost time.

"Eb, you go on back to the wagons and let 'em know what we're gonna do. I'll go 'head on an' find us a place to cut the ravine and make sure the wash'll be passable."

The former storekeeper nodded his head and reined his horse around to do as bidden. George pointed his gelding to the ravine, hopeful of an easy descent and a wide creek bottom for the wagons to make it to the Yellowstone before dark.

———

BAANI SANGLANT HAD CHOSEN WELL. The camp of the Black-foot renegades lay high up the eastern slope of the northern tip of the Absaroka Mountain Range. The flats of the Yellowstone valley stretched out to the east and north and the river bent back to the south and around the band of black-forested mountains, giving the renegades what they considered to be their prime hunting territory. But the game they sought was not native to the land, most were intruders and interlopers. Even though this land had been ceded to the Crow people by a treaty with the whites in 1851, none of the renegades felt it necessary to submit to what they considered to be a treasonous compromise with the lying whites. Nor did they believe the whites had any right or authority to dictate to the native peoples as to what territory belonged to which tribe or to the invaders with their strange beliefs about ownership of the land.

Although Baani and his friend, Four Horns, were the originators of the band of renegades, when Peenaquim brought four of his followers to join the band, he stood alongside Baani as a leader. It was at Baani's suggestion that Caleb be added to their band, and the big black man had repeatedly proven himself by showing his prowess in battle, earning him the status of a leader. The three leaders were seated around the fire, when their scout, Running Rabbit, told of his sighting.

"Three wagons, this many long ears," holding up two hands then adding four fingers, "and horses. Men have rifles, but do not watch. We showed ourselves, but they did not shoot or chase. Wagons are heavy with good, deep tracks."

The three leaders looked to one another, and Peenaquim asked, "Women?"

Rabbit shook his head, "We saw none."

Baani stood and looked at the scouts, "Trappers?"

The second scout, Wild Person, stepped forward, "None wore," fingering his buckskin vest, "skins like the trappers or hunters of the white men."

Caleb grunted, leaned to one side on an elbow, "That means they're pilgrims, settlers, wantin' to find gold or make farms." His face showed a sudden thought, "Were there any like me?" pointing to his skin.

"We saw none, we were not close to see in the wagons," added Wild Person, "their scouts looked to the big river. I think they will try to cross where the river has the sandbar in the middle. They will be at the river by dark."

Baani looked from Peenaquim to Caleb, or Black Bear, to see if they agreed. Both nodded their heads in agreement. Baani spoke to Running Rabbit and Wild Person, "Go, tell the others, we will ride to take these wagons!" The scouts looked to one another, grinning, and trotted off to tell the others and to prepare for their attack.

Some of the warriors that rode with the band in the beginning, had taken their plunder and returned to their villages. But others had joined the Renegades, wanting to gain their own honors and prizes. Now the band numbered eighteen, mostly young eager warriors with a few proven fighters among them. Most of the new men looked to Black Bear as the leader to follow for he had shown his fearless-ness, always going into the thick of the battle and emerging unscathed. Baani resented Black Bear and the men that followed him. Yet, knowing the big man as the best warrior of the band, Baani was determined to not let his jealousy show, at least until Black Bear was no longer needed.

The renegade band kept to the creek bottoms or dry ravines that led to the valley of the Yellowstone. Rabbit and Wild Person had been sent to scout the wagons, ensuring their route and expected campsite would be as anticipated. Baani looked over his shoulder to see the position of the sun, now moving to the western horizon. He calculated they would have ample daylight to position their ambush and make the attack. The band rode single file and moved quietly, spaced out enough to limit the dust behind them.

Black Bear was third in line with the band of renegades. He let his horse have his head as they moved at a fast walk through the deep ravine, and the easy gait and shuffling motion of the horse gave the big man time to ponder. He was remembering the time spent with the Blackfeet, it had only been a few weeks since he first joined the group, but there had been many fights and raids. There had been two ambushes against the Shoshoni, one against a hunting party of Crow, and four against different groups of white men. He thought back, remembering his wife and their time together, dreaming of a life of freedom in the mountains or even going on to California and starting anew. Although prominent in his memory, the image of her murder by the white hunters they thought were their friends, fueled his anger and bitterness against all men, even the natives that had been shown as enemies of their band of renegades, and had driven him on his killing rampage.

Bile rose in his throat as he remembered, and his lip curled in a snarl as he pictured more arrogant white men before them; men with no regard for the Indian through whose land they traveled, nor with any concern for others that fought for the freedom they abused. But as he thought, he realized he was repeatedly having to force himself into a fighting rage, and each time he entered into the battle, all he could see were the faces of those men that had assaulted his wife. Yet he knew the men of the wagons before them had nothing to do with his wife's death, and could possibly be good men, not deserving the death that was about to be brought upon them. He dropped his head to rid himself of these thoughts, and even argued with himself that all these men were just alike, and all deserved to be put to death.

They were intercepted by the returning scouts as Rabbit

rode to the front of the column of raiders to speak to Baani. "The wagons are in the wide dry creek-bed that leads to the river at the place of the sandbar."

Baani looked to Peenaquim and Caleb, both men now beside him. The band had made a raid against some trappers camped on the Yellowstone not far from where the wagons would be and Peenaquim said, "There is a wide sand-bank there and trees are thick along the bluff. It will be a good place for a fight. If I take some men to the far side, down-river, and you and some men upriver on this side, then Black Bear can have some on the island. We can attack from all sides." He looked to Baani and Black Bear for their answer.

Baani added, "Four Horns can also take some men and come from behind them."

"It is good!" declared Peenaquim, looking from Black Bear to Baani. Both the Blackfeet waited for Black Bear's response and when he nodded his head, the two men grinned saying, "It is good!"

————

GEORGE WAS ON ONE KNEE, dipping into the water for a handful to drink. As he lifted his hand to his mouth, he brought his eyes to the trees on the sandbar. "I'm thinkin' right here would be a good place to cross, don't you?" He turned to look at Ebenezer, still sitting in the saddle as his horse strained at the reins to dip his nose in the water.

"Yeah, look's good. From where I sit, yonder on across that stretch o' sand, the water looks like it ain't too deep. What with the river splittin' to go 'round that island, it makes it easier for us to cross. But, we gonna cross tonight or in the mornin'?"

George stood, looking around behind him and across the sandbar. He motioned to the wide sandy stretch behind him and answered, "I think we'd do best by campin' here an' crossin' in the morning." He stepped into his stirrup and swung a leg over his horse's rump, reined around, and started back up the draw. "Let's go point the wagons down the right draw an' make sure they don't get buried in the soft sand of that creek bottom."

ATOP THE BLUFF to their right and unseen by the men lay Running Rabbit and Wild Person, watching and listening. Rabbit understood English but did not hear all that was said by the white men. He turned to Wild Person motioning for them to go back to the band and report.

George Owen switched off with Grant Marshall and now sat on the seat of the first wagon, his wife Bertha at his side. Grant rode back the way George had come and led the wagons down the dry creek bed. Following George's wagon was Adolphe Petersen, who had served as scout on the left flank, and Melvin Hyatt as scout on the right flank. Two wagons followed the scouts, driven by Mangini and Schmidt and guarded by McCormick and Specht.

The two remaining scouts and Anthony Mangini brought up the rear.

George and Bertha were talking and laughing as the wagon came to the mouth of the ravine and the greenery of the wide river bottom of the Yellowstone revealed itself like the parting of a wide curtain to show the wonder of life. After many miles of dusty brown traveling, with the only break the brief parting of watercourses, this panorama shone before them like a paradise. Bertha put her hand to her mouth, gasping, and looked to George, "Oh, it's beautiful! Oh, and the water, it's so clear! Oh, George, we have to stop here. I have wanted a bath for so long, it will be heaven!"

George was busy turning the wagon for the mules to face

toward the river, planning for the other two wagons to form their usual half-circle with the opening towards the water, believing any attack would come from the bluffs and not the river. He stopped the wagon, stood in the seat to look back at the second and third wagons to direct them into place. He lifted his hand to signal just as an arrow buried itself in his back. Bertha had been looking at the water and didn't hear the arrow fly, but the grunt from her husband made her turn. Seeing the shaft protruding from his back, she caught her breath, frozen in fear. When she realized what happened, she saw George grab at the bow of the canvas top, and she screamed.

Caleb and three warriors rose from cover on the island and he fired at the man on horseback in the middle of the wagons. Grant Marshall grabbed at his chest as blood flowered through his fingers, he looked to the island and saw a giant of a black man and three Indians splashing through the water toward them. Grant grabbed at the pistol in his belt, brought it up and fired at one of the warriors beside the black man. He missed, cocked the Dragoon again, and snapped a shot at the same Indian, this time scoring a hit. Grant dropped from his saddle, leaned against the wagon and brought up his rifle, only to have it knocked to the side by the biggest black man he had ever seen. Grant's eyes widened, and he grabbed at his pistol, but he felt a blow at his beltline, looked to see the haft of a big knife protruding. He looked up into the eyes of Caleb, and with a raspy voice, "Why?" and slid down the side of the wagon, eyes wide and staring at nothing.

Rifle fire boomed all around, war cries echoed from the bluffs, and a thin cloud of smoke from the black powder rifles lay like a wispy blanket in the midst of the chaos. Peenaquim and his four warriors struck the wagons from the trees, their first volley was followed by arrows and the charge as all five screaming, war-club wielding warriors assaulted the wagon with Bertha Owen firing her husband's Dragoon pistol. Two men fell to her fire, before she was dragged from the wagon by Peenaquim. The other warriors ran towards the second wagon where Jesse McCormick was in a face-to-face fight with Running Rabbit.

Baani Sanglant was sided by four fighters as they charged the third wagon and the rear guards. Michael and Anthony Mangini stood side by side, Anthony frantically trying to reload his Hawken while Michael fired at the charging Blackfeet with his Paterson Colt. Just as Baani was almost to the wagon, a sudden barrage from the rocks at the mouth of the ravine made him and the two beside him, drop to the sand. They expected one or two shots, believing the men would have to reload. When they looked up, saw no one, and started to rise, another blast from the nearest rock knocked the Blackfoot warrior back into Baani, putting them both on the sand. Baani looked at his companion, whose face had been obliterated by the buckshot from the Colt shotgun in the hands of Ebenezer Hardy, and with a quick glance to the rocks, Baani rolled under the wagon for cover. Hardy emptied the shotgun into the crowd of screaming Indians, dropped it to his side and picked up his carbine to search for another target. His hands were shaking as he tried to take aim, then lowered the carbine to rest on the rock, wiped his hands dry and brought it up again. But the sudden smack to his forehead knocked him backwards from the rock, and he was flattened, arms to the side, rifle clattering in the rocks, as blood welled from the single hole in his forehead.

The rampage was a maelstrom of confusion. War cries from the attackers, gun shots, shouts of agony and fright, brayed screams from panicked mules, and the rattle of trace chains as the mules fought their harness, blended into a cacophony of discordance that mocked the usual quiet of the chuckling river and the peace of the woods.

Melvin Hyatt had taken cover under the second wagon and began to take a toll on the charging Indians with his Sharps rifle. His first target was the leader of the four men on horseback as they charged down the ravine toward the wagons. The big Sharps boomed and the first rider, Four Horns, took the slug in his chest, somersaulting him over the rump of his horse. Hyatt dropped the lever to lower the block and reload with a paper cartridge. He hurriedly loaded, closed the breech, placed the cap on the nipple, cocked the hammer to set the triggers, and brought it up to his cheek to take aim. The charging Indians were almost on him when he fired again and as he looked through the smoke, he saw his targeted warrior on the ground, unmoving. Starting to reload, he was surprised when a tomahawk from Baani struck him from the side, burying the blade across his nose and in his eyes. Hyatt's face was instantly covered with blood as he dropped into the sand.

There was a moment of silence, but as the attackers realized the battle was over, their war cries sounded loud and long as they began taking scalps and rummaging through the wagons. Every white man was dead and seven of the attackers were killed. Caleb walked among the dead, looking at the carnage, fighting the desire to turn away and vomit. He tried to rationalize that these men had probably been slaveholders and worse. But he didn't know, he wasn't certain, and he argued with himself that these men were invaders and thieves, coming where they weren't wanted and taking what was not theirs.

He walked the half-circle of wagons and was approaching the river when he came to the first wagon in line. Laying on the sand beside the wagon was the body of a white woman. Her clothing had been ripped away, her scalp taken, and her body had been mutilated. She was covered with blood and sand, and even if he had known her, he would not have been able to recognize her. He could hold it no longer and ran to the water's edge to empty his guts into the river. He splashed water on his face and neck, again and again, wanting to wash away even the memory of what he saw, but it would not leave him. He shook his head as he knelt on one knee on the wet sand, remembering what his mother had always told him about respecting a woman, no matter what color her skin. Killing the men was one thing, but killing a woman? He pictured his mother sitting beside the woman of the house where she worked as a cook, the wife of the man who owned her and her children, but who was considered a friend of his mother. He breathed deep and stood to return to the slaughter and the men he had chosen to ride with, renegades every one. He thought of himself as a renegade, but not a murderer. Or was he?

CHAPTER EIGHTEEN
CROW

PEENAQUIM SAT ACROSS THE FIRE FROM BAANI, GAVE A sweeping motion with his hand, "We are in Crow country, they are our enemies!"

Baani scowled at the man, "We go where we want, we spit on the Apsáalooke!"

The Piegan leader's forehead wrinkled and his eyes narrowed, "Four summers past, the leaders of the Crow put their mark on the white man's paper at Horse Creek. The white man said that gave this land to the Crow until the sun no longer shines. When the leaders of the Blackfeet gave their mark on the paper with the white man Stevens, this summer past, our leaders agreed for our people to have the land beyond the Musselshell River. The Crow have many warriors and they are fierce fighters. If we are found here, they will come against us with more than we have."

Baani's eyes were pinched to slits and the edge of his lip lifted as he glared at Peenaquim. "Peenaquim is afraid! Where is the man that charged into the white men, screaming his war cry as he brought death to the men that stink?"

"The weak and cowardly white men are nothing! But to

face a Crow band that would have five warriors for every one of ours? That is not weak, that is," as he slapped the side of his head, "foolish!"

"The Crow have not seen us, they do not know we are here," answered Baani, but his tone was uncertain as he looked at Peenaquim. His expression as he turned his head slightly away but kept his eyes on the Piegan, wondering if he knew more.

"Our scouts have seen sign of someone watching our camp. Three riders," pointing to the upper slope of the mountainside, "there."

Baani jumped to his feet, looked in the direction of Peenaquim's pointing, back at the man and said, "We will leave!" He looked around, calculating where to go, and grinned as he glared at Peenaquim, "We will go to the land of the Snake! Where the water thunders!" He smiled as he thought, "We will take women from them. With our many horses and prizes, we will return to our land and have our own village!"

Peenaquim, now standing, grinned at the idea of women and a village of their own. They had taken many horses, weapons and other prizes. They would be respected as a village of strong warriors with many goods.

THE CAMP of the Blackfeet renegades, in the northern reaches of the Absaroka range, although convenient for them, was in the Crow territory. This land had been assigned to the Crow by the 1851 Fort Laramie treaty, called the Horse Creek treaty by the natives. Many tribes, including the Lakota Sioux, Cheyenne, Crow, Arapaho, Arikara, Assiniboine, Hidatsa and Mandan had signed, agreeing to the terms. But the Blackfeet had refused to be a part and the renegades under Baani fought against such treaties

A later treaty, called the Stevens Treaty of 1855, was an amendment to the Laramie treaty and ascribed territories to the many tribes of the confederation of the Blackfeet. It was the signing of that treaty that prompted the rebellion of many of the Blackfeet whose bands and leaders had not signed. Both treaties required the different tribes to halt hostilities with one another and with the whites, including those passing through their lands, and to have common hunting grounds. It was the excuse needed by young warriors like Baani Sanglant, who sought honors and plunder that could not be gained if the treaties were honored. The Blackfoot territory was north of the Musselshell River, well north of the camp of the renegades. But both these treaties were broken by inter-tribal fighting within months of signing and by whites that ignored all the tenants of the agreements.

————

WHEN THE CROW HUNTING PARTY, led by Twists His Tail, returned to the village with only two elk, the villagers fell silent, knowing the meat would only provide a couple days fare for the people. With ten of the villages' best hunters, everyone expected to see the horses weighed down with meat for all the people. Twists His Tail slipped from his mount as he neared the lodge of the village leader, Bull Chief. The chief, seeing the look of defeat on Twists His Tail's face and his drooped shoulders, motioned for the leader of the hunting party to enter his lodge.

Both men were seated, opposite one another, with the coals from the nights fire between them, as Bull Chief simply said, "Speak."

"There are Blackfeet in the mountains, there!" Twists His Tail pointed to the north where they had their hunt.

Bull Chief leaned forward, alarm and anger showing on his face. "Where?!"

"On the last of the mountains that look to the river of the Yellowstone. They had many rifles and horses, this many warriors," he flashed all the fingers of both hands twice, "and more!"

"Did they see you?"

"No. We had split our hunters to find more game. Three of our men saw the camp from above and were hidden from them. We came back with only two elk to tell you of these raiders in our lands."

"You did good." The chief sat silent and still, eyes staring into the coals, as he considered the threat presented. After several moments, he looked up to Twists His Tail, "You, take three men, watch the camp of the Blackfeet. We will meet in the valley below the last mountain that sits between the rivers that go north." Tail knew the place described, rose and with a nod to his chief, left the lodge.

Bull Chief called for his woman, instructed her to summon the other leaders and elders of the village to his lodge. Within moments, several men were seated around the firepit facing their chief. Bull looked around the circle, then growled, "Our enemies, the Blackfeet, have come into our lands! Our hunters saw their camp in the mountains to the north. They had many horses and rifles and four hands of warriors! They are not hunting; they are raiding!"

The men of the circle made many exclamations and beat the ground with their fists. White Crane, a recognized war leader, spoke, "We must go against them before they come to our village!"

The others nodded and voiced their agreement. Two Leggings, the shaman of the village, added, "The Blackfeet must be driven from our land. They will try to take our women and more!"

"Aiiieeee," rose the cry from many of the leaders, others shouting their own war cry.

Bull Chief asked, "Do we agree? We must drive these Blackfeet from our land?" He looked from man to man around the circle of the leaders, each one answering with a head nod or by hitting his fist to the ground. As he completed the circle, he directed, "I will lead our warriors! White Crane, Two Leggings, and Long Hair, you will gather three hands of warriors each. We will leave when the sun is high!" Again, shouts and war cries sounded among the men as they hurried from the lodge to prepare for their assault.

————

It is an unseen gap that separates arrogance and confidence. A man of confidence has usually gained such by succeeding, whether it is in battle or other contests, but he also knows that success was not entirely of his own doing. While a man with arrogance claims his success is totally of his own doing, and often looks with disdain on those he sees as subordinates. And often the arrogant man will grow careless, believing himself to be invincible. These were the words that echoed in Caleb's mind as he looked at Baani and Peenaquim. The words told Caleb by his one white friend, the man who had given him his manumission papers, had been words that helped in the making of Caleb the man, yet now they were words he used to measure the men he now followed.

Caleb watched Baani look with contempt at his own followers. He had shown his arrogance after the last battle with the white men at the wagons. He strutted around with his trophy scalps and derided those that had been killed or wounded. Caleb dropped his eyes as the leader shouted, "If you had been like me, we would not have lost so many! You are weak! You are like children that play games! Now we go to find the Shoshoni to take women but if you cannot fight even these poor Snakes, you do not need a woman!" Baani ran to his tethered horse, a quick hop and he swung aboard. Waving his war club over his head, "We go!" he kicked his horse and the big bay leaped forward as his rider screamed his war cry.

Running Rabbit had been given the task of riding point for the herd of horses driven by the others. The herd was the wealth of the raiders, as horses were used as currency was to a white man. It was with horses that a man showed his prowess as a warrior, or to pay a bride price, or to add to the status of the village. And their goal was to have their own village. Once they neared the land of the Shoshoni, they would leave the herd under the guard of a few warriors while the proven fighters would make the attack. But the land of the Snake people was at least two-or-three days ride for the renegades, all within Crow territory.

Mid-morning of the third day, one of the out-rider scouts came at a gallop toward the renegade band as they drove the herd. Black Shell shouted the warning, "Crow! They have seen us!"

Baani and Peenaquim waved the man to a stop. Baani asked, "Where are they?"

Shell turned and pointed to a timbered draw coming from the mountainside, "There!"

"How soon?" asked Peenaquim.

The scout turned again, pointing, "There, the dust!" No more than a couple of miles away, a cloud of dust rose that could only be from a large group of riders moving fast.

Peenaquim, ever the strategist, started barking orders. He looked to the scout, "Shell, take three, go there," pointing to a low rising ridge to his left, "wait until they charge, then you attack!" He motioned to another, "Red Crow, you, three more, go!" he pointed to a thick cluster of juniper on the downhill side on the right.

After the fight at the wagons the number of the renegades had been depleted by a third and now numbered only twelve. Baani and Black Bear looked at Peenaquim expectantly as he added, "We will run the horses at them! If we get through, we can attack from behind!" Baani and Caleb looked to one another, nodded, and moved away from Peenaquim, spacing the three about five or six feet apart, yet behind the herd. Because they had been moving slowly through the scattered trees, the herd had not stirred up much of a dust cloud. The three men looked to the dust beyond and saw the Crow warriors starting to spread out for their attack. Peenaquim looked to the others, raised his rifle over his head and shouted his war cry! The herd moved as if all were connected and leaped forward, stretching out as the men behind shouted and screamed. Rabbit was surprised but kicked his horse into a gallop and led the herd directly at the attackers.

The Crow, led by Big Chief, were startled and reined their horses to the side to avoid the stampeding herd. The charging animals split the attacking force, and Rabbit, holding his Hawken with one hand, lowered the barrel and fired point-blank at the nearest Crow, knocking him from his mount to be trampled by the stampeding herd. Rabbit screamed his war-cry as he passed, waving his rifle at another Crow. Yet he had made but a few lengths before a Crow warrior swung a long, heavy-headed war club that caught Rabbit in the middle of his chest and unseated him to land in front of the charging herd.

Caleb was shrouded in the thick dust cloud and lay along the neck of the big black horse, mane slapping his face, as through squinted eyes he saw the throng of attackers. He swung the barrel of his rifle around, fired the .54 caliber ball at the startled face of a charging Crow, and obliterated the screaming visage. He lay the Hawken across the black's withers, grasping it with a handful of mane in his left hand. He snatched up the big Dragoon pistol and cut loose on the crowd of screaming Crow. One fell, another slumped on the neck of his horse, another grabbed at his chest, others ducked or slid to the far side of their mounts. When the hammer fell on an empty chamber, Caleb was past the attackers. He jabbed the Colt into his belt and leaned down to urge his horse on into the thickening trees.

The cacophony of carnage ratcheted across the wide ravine, echoes bouncing between the granite topped mountains. Screams of war cries and agony were interspersed with rifle fire and the thunder of hooves. Dust and powder smoke masked the mélange of madness as the diminishing sounds of battle were filtered by the pines.

Caleb and company were less concerned about the herd of horses than their own escape. To turn and fight would be suicidal and any of their number left behind would never leave the mountainside. Caleb sat upright on the black stallion and searched the trees for sign of survivors. He kept the horse at a canter, giving him time to catch his breath after the long running escape, and the first man he saw was Peenaquim, slumped over the neck of his horse. Caleb pulled up to wait for the man, grabbed the reins of the horse to stop him beside his black.

Peenaquim tried to sit upright, saw the face of Caleb showing concern, and with a motion to his left shoulder, "I was cut by a Crow's hawk! He will cut no more!" he muttered in a snarl and dropped back to his mount's neck, grasping a handful of mane.

Mid-afternoon saw a small herd of horses managed by four men, Caleb, Baani, Peenaquim and Red Crow, stop in a grassy clearing beside a wide swath of Aspen. Just below the edge of the trees lay the valley of the Yellowstone, now coming from the south. The men slid from their horses, led them to the small stream with the others and let the herd drink, knowing they were too tired to do more than graze on the nearby grass. The four survivors of the Crow attack found shade and stretched out for their own rest.

CHAPTER NINETEEN
OBSERVATION

IN THE MIDST OF THE BLACK TIMBER, ONE TREE-TOP SHOOK back and forth, seemingly of its own volition. The lightning-struck towering spruce showed a split top with a dead snag protruding through the green canopy. At its base, a massive silver-tip grizzly was doing the dance of the bears, scratching his back up and down on the broken limb stubs and the gnarly bark. Above his head were the deep claw marks that warned other bears that this was his territory. He stretched his nose to the air and sniffed without missing a step in his back-scratching ballet. He dropped to all fours, rubbing his rear end against the trunk for both a last massage and to leave his scent. Satisfied, he lumbered off to the thicker woods to find his bed.

If a man were to ride past this storm marked tree, he would have to stand in his stirrups and stretch to his highest reach to touch the bottom of the claw marks. And it was in this position that Tate found Knuckles as he rode up behind him. The old man dropped into his saddle, turned back to look at his friend, "Ain't never seen one that big afore! You?"

"He's a big 'un alright, and those marks are fresh!" answered Tate, leaning forward for a better look.

"I kin smell 'im too!" added Knuckles, wrinkling his nose.

"Me too!" said Maggie, pulling up beside Tate. Within moments, the entire group was gathered near the claw-marked tree and each one had to add their comments.

"Will he come after us, Pa?" chimed Sadie.

Tate chuckled as he dropped back into his saddle to look to his youngest, "No, sweetheart, I don't think he'll be coming our way. But just to be safe, Knuckles is gonna looksee where that bear went off to, and we'll go the other way! How's that?"

"Oh, I wasn't scared. I thought I might get to shoot him with my new Hawken!" Sadie had been given one of the rifles left over from the trade goods and was quite proud of her first weapon. It made her feel so grown-up. Sean and her pa had shown her how to load and shoot the rifle, although it was a little heavy for her to handle. But she had learned to use whatever was near as a shooting rest and had repeatedly proven her skill measured up to the rest of her family.

Sean snorted as he commented, "By the time you got that rifle ready, everyone else would already have put it down!"

"Now Sean, you might want to watch what you say, she can handle that thing pretty well, you know," cautioned Maggie. "I'd hate to see her turn it on her big brother."

"Oh, Ma, I wouldn't do that! I might chuck a rock or two at him, but I wouldn't shoot him!" declared the girl, with a very serious expression.

Knuckles climbed back aboard and turned toward the others, "Looks like he done took off up the mountain thar," pointing with the muzzle of his rifle toward a break in the timber. "So if'n we keep goin' like we was headed, down yonder ways," he nodded his head toward the valley bottom, "he'll be long gone away from us."

"Sounds good to me," answered Tate, lifting his eyes to the

lowering sky, "looks like we'll get there before dark, so we can make us a good camp. Might even catch us some fish for supper, whaddaya think Sean?"

"Ummm, I can already taste 'em, Pa!"

The caravan had crossed the wide bald plateau and dropped into the timber on the broad shoulders of the far-reaching upland. They held to a well-used game trail that also showed sign of hunting parties, probably from the Shoshoni and Nez Perce. The bear tree was on a side-slope where the trail overlooked a wide ravine with clusters of aspen and willows. Knuckles led the way as they came to the edge of the tree line where the twisting Snake river carved its way toward the big lake in the shadow of the Tetons.

Knuckles waited for Tate to come alongside and asked, "So, ya think it'd be better to stay back in the trees, or ya wanna go down by the river an' be in the open?"

Tate surveyed the area before them, turned to look back into the trees and upon seeing a couple of clearings nearby, he nodded toward them, "Let's stay in the trees here. We can stake the horses in the grass or near the water an' bring 'em back to that clearing an' picket 'em for the night."

Knuckles nodded agreement, "Sounds good to me. Ain't particular, long's we get a chance to put on the feedbag. I'm so hungry, muh belly-button's pinchin' muh backbone!"

With a chuckle, Tate turned to motion to the others where to go and he reined Shady toward the clearing. It was a well-practiced routine to set up camp and they made short work of the task. Soon, the cookfire was blazing, Maggie and Pinaquanah were busy at readying the evening meal. Tate and Knuckles were tending the horses, staking them within reach of water and tall grass, and Sean and Sadie at the water's edge, trying to catch some trout for supper.

The Snake River made a sharp bend to the west, was joined by a smaller mountain run-off creek, and turned back to the south. The camp was nearer the smaller stream and hidden from view in the tall pines. But the grass that beckoned the horses and the men that led them, was in the open and with deep grass waving in the cool breeze as the men staked out their prized animals.

On the opposite side of the Snake River, the timber covered slope staggered up to the base of a long ridge that caught the last blaze of the setting sun. In the cluster of juniper that hung tenuously on the edge of the ridge, sat three men astraddle their horses. They watched the miniscule figures that led the horses into the grass and grinned at their recognition of the brightly marked horses of the Nez Perce. Peenaquim pointed his finger as he counted, then turned to Baani, "There are two hands and two, but not all are the Nez Perce ponies."

Baani and Caleb leaned on the withers of their horses as they watched the activity below. Suddenly Baani sat up, pointing, "Women! That one has fire in her hair!" He grinned as he watched the two women walking side-by-side to the smaller stream where the two youngsters were fishing.

"Ho! The girl also has flaming hair!" declared the renegade when he saw the girl embrace the woman. "We will take them and the horses!" declared the leader of the small band. "Those horses are great prizes and that woman will warm my blankets with her fiery hair!"

Caleb sat quietly, watching those below and looking back to the men he rode with, and dropped his eyes to the mane of his horse. He had said nothing about the killing of the white woman; when he found her there was nothing to be said, but he remembered her mutilated body. He thought of his own wife and what the white trappers had done that enraged him. But his turning renegade did not wipe out his memory of his mother's teaching about respecting women. A man should always protect and respect women and the thought of taking a white woman, any woman, captive, and taking her from her children, brought bile into his throat and he breathed heavily, shaking his head slightly as his mind churned.

His anger against the white man had been sated and he was thinking more clearly. These men that now rode beside him did not hold to the same beliefs. They even argued with one another, both seemingly blinded to the right and wrong of things, thinking only of their material gain. *Is it not always so among men when greed overwhelms conscience?*

Red Crow joined the three watchers and answered the questioning look of Baani with, "The horses are safe in the canyon, as you said."

Baani nodded, looked to the others, and with a swift motion, kicked his horse toward the game trail that led to the bottom of the valley. They moved cautiously and silently through the lofty pines, picking every step carefully, always searching through any break in the trees for a view of the park where the white men's horses grazed. The sun had dipped below the western hills when the four broke from the tree line near the bank of the Snake River. They slid from their mounts and drew together to frame their plan.

"They have many horses, it will be easy to take them!" suggested Red Crow.

"These horses will be a fine prize, but we cannot lose any more men," said Peenaquim, looking at Baani, who was nervously pacing back and forth among the cluster of trees.

"We will not lose any men! These are few and we can take them before they know we are there!"

"These are not foolish or careless men and they will not be easy to take, with these horses and the women, the men will be watchful and well-armed," injected Black Bear.

Peenaquim agreed with Black Bear and referred to him by his Blackfoot name, "Sik kiáá yo speaks true. We must choose if we want the horses or the women, not both."

"I want the women and the horses! We will take both!" demanded Baani, stepping closer to Peenaquim.

"We must scout the camp, see if there is a way we can do both," suggested Black Bear.

Red Crow quickly added, "Black Bear is right! I will scout the camp, then we will decide!"

"That is best!" stated Peenaquim. He looked to the darkening sky and added, "We will wait . . . and two will scout. Then we decide."

Baani didn't like Peenaquim's demand, but the others stood by the man and faced Baani, waiting for his agreement. The renegade let out a heavy breath, hit his balled fist against his thigh and growled, "We will scout! Sik Kiáá yo will scout with me!"

Peenaquim knew Baani and believed the arrogance of the man demanded some small success in this debate and he nodded his agreement. He stepped back to find a place of comfort to wait. He was joined by Red Crow, who had been of a different band of the Blackfeet but one of the followers when they first joined Baani's band of cutthroats. Black Bear walked off by himself to lean against a tall ponderosa and look to the river that chuckled its way around the bend toward the small park area that held the spotted ponies. The former slave absent-mindedly grabbed a handful of the tall grasses at his side and picked at them as he thought. He would go with Baani to see the camp of the whites, but he had reservations about attacking them. His heart still ached for his wife, Beatrice, but his anger at her death had been tempered with the deaths of the many white men. But he was still bothered about the death of the white woman. He had begun to think of himself as a man without a people. He could no longer find a place in white civilization with his freedom still in doubt because he had stolen his papers. And the white men of the mountains had shown themselves to be too willing to deal death to all that didn't live according to their ways, regardless of their skin color. Some of the natives, to his surprise, seemed willing to accept him as a man no matter their differences. But he had yet to find anyplace or people that fully accepted him with no expectations or need for him to prove himself by killing others.

He shook his head and let his memories of his young-adulthood flood into his mind. Those years, when he served with his wife and mother in the household of the man that offered them freedom with the manumission papers, were also the years of learning. In that home he was taught to read and cipher and to appreciate having his eyes opened to the world through the pages of literature. Even though still in slavery, he believed those were the best years of his life. But he also knew he had many years before him and the choices made, perhaps in these next few days, would dictate what his life would become.

"Mama, when you were my age, did you go to school?" implored Sadie, looking across the fire at her ma and pa sitting together, with steaming cups of coffee cupped in their hands. Everyone was gathered by the fire as the star-studded night sky canopied the wilderness camp. Campfires gave moments of reflection, times of sharing, and quiet interludes of introspection. Sadie and her ma had often spoken about learning and education, and Maggie took advantage of every opportunity to turn common questions into learning experiences.

"Yes, I did. Because my father was a first mate on a sailing ship, he brought my mother back from Spain to Ireland where I was born. We lived in a small village and we had a school with only one teacher for all the grades. But it was a special experience and that was where I first learned to love reading and understanding the many things of the world."

"How old were you when you came to America?"

"A little older than your brother is now, I was thirteen. We moved west with whatever work my father could find, and when he came to the mountains, my Mum and I stayed behind. But after my Mum died, I came out west to look for your grandpa and, as I've told you before, that's when I met your pa and we started our family."

"I think I'd like to go to a school like you did and learn everything like you!" declared the innocent girl, poking at the fire with a long willow stick.

Maggie lifted her eyebrows, looked to Tate with a side-long glance, and back to the little redhead. Before she could respond to her daughter, her thoughts were interrupted by Sean.

"Not me! I ain't interested in no school!" pooching his lips out as he leaned back against the smooth boulder. "I can learn all I need right'chere, right Pa?"

"That's *I'm not interested in any school!*" corrected his mother and added, "And the way you're talking, you could use some proper education!"

"Awww, Ma. Alright, I'm not interested in any school. But I still think I can learn all I need to know out here in the mountains! Pa did!"

"No, that's not right, son. My father was a school teacher and I had a proper education all the time I was growing up. My father gave me an education that was even more than I could have received if I went to a college. He was always teaching me, and I've tried, apparently not hard enough, to pass that on to you!" answered Tate.

Knuckles chuckled at the exchange and chimed in, "Younker, I ain't never had much eddycation, but that shore don't mean I ain't wisht I had. There's lots o' things you cain't learn out'chere in the mountains, things ya' only find in books!"

Pinaquanah leaned against her husband, looking to the youngsters, "Even among my people, we teach our young. We have times when the elders gather the children and tell the stories that begin with our creation story. Then another will tell of coyote the trickster and the many other ways we use to tell our young about our people. It is much like your school."

"I'd like to hear those stories," chimed Sadie, wide-eyed as she looked to Smells of Sugar.

Sugar looked around the circle of expectant expressions and began, "Well, there is one about coyote, or A pe' si." She began to relate the story of how Old Man had been lonely and used some left-over bones and created men for company. When he breathed smoke into their eyes, they came to life and went to the fire to sit and smoke. But when A pe'si came back, he saw more left-over bones and suggested Old Man make more company, and A pe'si helped. This time when Old Man breathed smoke into their eyes, they sat around and talked. "And so you see, to this day, whenever people come together, the men sit by the fire and smoke, and the women join together and talk. That is because A pe'si, who is a noisy creature himself, had a part in their making."

Sadie started clapping her hands as she said, "Oh, Sugar! That is a great story!"

"Yes, it was, but I think it's time we all go to our blankets. We still have a long way to go before we get to the village," instructed Maggie as she stood to hustle the youngsters to their bedrolls.

Tate stood, motioned to Knuckles, and spoke to the women, "We're gonna get the horses settled in and we'll be right back."

Maggie gave a wave of her hand as she hurried Sadie and Sean toward the lean-to shelter. Sugar followed Maggie but turned to the separate lean-to for her and Big Fist to prepare the hides and blankets for their night.

As Tate and Knuckles walked from the trees, Tate lifted his eyes to the stars and commented, "Looks like some clouds are movin' down from the north. Might get a little cold tonight, maybe even a little wet."

Knuckles did his own survey of the night sky and agreed, "Ummmhummm, prob'ly so."

As they neared the tethered horses, each one on a long lead to provide ample graze, they pulled the stakes and gathered the leads, each man taking three horses. Tate suggested, "I think we'll picket the appaloosas in that small clearing next to the creek, an' we'll put the others in the bigger clearing closer to camp."

"Sounds reasonable. That crick yonder's known as Polecat Crick, but I ain't never seen a polecat 'round it, so, I don't think them horses'd be bothered none. With our reg'lar horses near camp, they can warn us if anythin' comes around."

"That's what I was thinkin', 'course I've always got Lobo nearby, but I'd feel better with the horses close at hand."

"Yeppir, me too," agreed Knuckles.

They soon had the appaloosas, including the leopard spotted packhorse, on a picket line at the edge of the trees by the stream. The tautly stretched rope provided a tether for the halter leads of each of the appaloosas, keeping them well secured and close to one another for company. The other horses were also put on a picket line but nearer the camp, within sight of their lean-tos.

When Tate and Knuckles came back to the camp, the coals glowed in the fire pit and the others were in their blankets. The men crawled under the covers, keeping their rifles and handguns near at hand. Tate stroked the head of Lobo who lay at his side and he looked to the youngsters with Indy laying on their feet, sharing the warmth. He rolled to his back to see past the edge of the lean-to for a look at the sky. The storm clouds were slowly sliding to the south drawing a curtain of black across the heavens. Tate rolled to his side, touched the face of his redhead and let sleep take him.

"I THINK it would be best for Peenaquim and Red Crow to do the scout. Both are better at moving quietly in the night than I am," declared Black Bear as he stood beside Baani. "It would not be good for me to give us away in the dark."

Baani looked at the big black man who stood head and shoulders above him, looked to Peenaquim and nodded, "You and Crow will make the scout. We will wait by the river for you before we decide to take the horses and women."

Peenaquim, or Seen From Afar, was glad to make the scout. He did not trust Baani to scout without trying to take the women, plus he had thought of a better plan. He motioned for Baani and Black Bear to come near and he began to share his thoughts about the white men and their horses and women. As Peenaquim outlined his plan, he watched Baani grin and nod his head in agreement. When Seen From Afar finished, he leaned back and waited for Baani or Black Bear to comment.

"It is a good plan, and I feel you are right about what the white men will do. The women will be a better prize than the rest of the horses!" answered Baani, looking to Black Bear for him to agree.

Black Bear had listened closely, thinking all the while about other possibilities, and when the others looked to him for his answer, he nodded his head, "It is a good plan."

Peenaquim and Red Crow left their horses and rifles with Baani and Caleb and waded into the cold waters of the Snake River. Once across, Peenaquim lifted his eyes to the dark canopy, pointed out the storm clouds to Red Crow and whispered, "That will give us cover." He trotted off to the trees without waiting for a response. Crow followed closely as they kept inside the tree line, padding their way quietly on the pine needle carpeted game trail. They passed the camp, staying well back in the thick timber as they worked around to the tethered horses. As they neared the clearing, they dropped to the ground and slowly made their way closer, any noise they made was covered by the rising breeze that preceded the coming storm.

———

THE LOW GROWL from Lobo confirmed Tate's concerns and he searched the camp and the tree line moving only his eyes as he gripped the rifle stock beside him. He saw the horses all looking into the trees, ears forward, as they too searched for any signs of danger. Something had alerted them, but they showed no nervousness and Tate thought it could be anything, including Indians. He rolled from his blankets, slowly rising at the side of the lean-to, careful to not let his shadowy silhouette give away his presence. Once he was certain whatever it was that had alerted the horses was not near, he started to the tree line, Lobo matching him step for step.

As he neared the second clearing where the appaloosas were tethered, he paused to listen. Although the cicadas had fallen silent for a while, their ratcheting sounds began again, easing the tension felt by Tate. The horses stood hipshot and silent, only the leopard spotted packhorse looked his way, probably picking up his scent. Tate looked at Lobo and watched the wolf as he carefully searched the area with his piercing eyes. Occasionally, his head would drop just a mite, and he would look and use all his senses as he searched. When the wolf visibly relaxed, Tate touched his scruff and turned back to the camp, "Maybe it was just the wind and comin' storm, Lobo. I was thinkin' it might be that grizz, but the horses woulda been more upset if it was. Let's go get us some sleep, boy."

————

"THAT MAN HAD A WOLF BESIDE HIM!" whispered Red Crow as he watched the white man disappear into the trees.

"He is not like other men. He will be dangerous. We will wait before we go to the horses," replied Peenaquim in a whisper. The two relaxed in the deep darkness of the trees, comfortable on the deep bed of pine needles.

The ragged bolts of lightning appeared to walk down the mountains like a glowing skeleton of spirits past, bones rattling and disjointed, each step shaking the earth itself. Thunder clapped a cadence of echoes that bounced between the granite peaks and vibrated the trees. When the water came it was anticlimactic. The wind whipped the rain through the pines and aspen and refused to release its grip on each raindrop until every side of every rock and tree was soaked.

Peenaquim and Red Crow rose from a crouch and spoke to the horses as they approached. The sound of voices brought a semblance of comfort to the drenched animals and any sound that was made was lost in the cacophony of the storm. The men cut the tethers, slipped aboard a horse, and with the leads of the others in hand, they started walking to the river. Once away from the clearing, it was just a short distance to the river and they didn't hesitate at water's edge, knowing the storm waters would swell the river soon and they had to cross before that came. These were Indian ponies and were responsive to their riders. The crossing was without difficulty and the two were met by the anxious Baani and Caleb.

Peenaquim slipped to the ground and spoke to Baani, "The white man has a wolf and is a man of the woods. He will be dangerous. When he came to the horses, I followed him back to the camp and saw there is one other man, two women, and two children. They will not know we have the horses until after the storm. We will wait until the rain stops, then we will go so the man can follow the tracks."

CHAPTER TWENTY-ONE
SEPARATION

TATE SAT QUIET AS HE WATCHED THE BEGINNING OF COLOR make silhouettes of the jagged eastern mountain range before the sunrays bent to touch the western mountains behind him. His favorite time of the day was to observe the artist creator paint the first moments of each dawn and to spend his customary time in prayer. He sat atop a rocky crag that jutted out from most of the surrounding trees and over-looked the bend of the Snake River, but the towering spruce and pine obscured his view of the clearings and the camp. He stood and stretched, stepped down from his perch, and picked his way through the trees to the camp.

Tate had stirred the coals and added some wood to the fire before he went to the mountain, and as he returned he saw his redhead fiddling with the coffeepot and readying things for their breakfast. "Mornin' beautiful!" he declared as he walked up behind her. She stood and turned, smiling broadly, "Morning. Coffee'll be ready soon, and those duck eggs Sean found yesterday will start the day off right for us, don'tcha think?"

Tate grinned and with his hands at her waist, drew

Maggie close for an early taste of his favorite breakfast. She wrapped her arms around his neck and kissed him, leaned back and smiled adding, "My, aren't we romantic this morning."

He chuckled, gave her a big hug, and stepped back to reach for the coffee pot. When he touched the hot handle, he snatched his hand back, and looked for the usual scrap of buckskin used to pick up the hot pots. Maggie grinned at him, "That's what you get for being so anxious." She extended the buckskin pot-holder to him with one hand and a cup with the other. He poured the cup full of the steaming brew, accepted the second cup, and filled it. They sat together on the grey log and enjoyed the closeness and the few moments of being together without the others.

"We should make it to the village by late today, then it'll only be a few days and we'll be back home," surmised Tate, sipping his coffee.

"I've enjoyed our time and we've seen a lot. It's been good for the kids to see those geysers and such, not very many would ever have the chance."

Tate looked at Maggie and said, "I think I hear a 'but' coming."

She gave him a wistful smile, "But I can't help thinking about Sadie and schooling. Sean loves it here and you have taught him a lot, but Sadie . . . " she let the thought hang in the air between them.

Tate drew a deep breath, swallowed the rest of the coffee, threw the dregs in the fire and stood. "While you get breakfast, I'll go bring in the other horses."

Maggie looked up at Tate, knowing that was his way when he didn't want to talk about something, to find some other task to take him away. But she also knew he would think about what was said and take his time considering everything he could before approaching the thought again.

She tiptoed to peck him on the cheek, "Alright, I'll get things started."

Maggie had cooked the pork belly and was almost finished with the eggs when she looked up to see Tate walking quickly into the clearing. She looked to Pinaquanah and back to Tate who was obviously troubled about something, "What's the matter?"

Tate looked at her and at Knuckles, who approached the fire with an empty coffee cup. "They're gone. The appaloosas are gone."

"Was it that grizz?" asked Knuckles, starting to reach for his rifle.

"Not unless he had a knife! The picket line was cut!" answered Tate, showing the end of the rope that had been tied off at the tree. He tossed the scrap to the ground and looked to Knuckles, "What with the storm, they got away clean. I looked all around for tracks, but there was no sign to show much of anything. But the string of horses left enough of a trail to point to the river. We can probably pick up a trail 'cross the water."

"Then let's get a move on!" declared Knuckles snatching up his rifle and turning toward the horses.

"Let's get some food down first, it might be a long chase."

Knuckles turned back to look at Tate, glanced at the pork belly snapping in the pan and the eggs that stared back, rubbed his belly, "You don't have to ask me twicet!"

As they ate, Tate was thinking and planning, and looked up at Maggie, "We don't know how many there are, and I'd feel a lot better if you and the kids were safe back at the village." He looked to Knuckles, "Whaddayou think, old man?"

"Old man? Thar ya go insultin' me agin! But, I agree. I think it would be best for Sugar to take 'em back to the village, providin' them hoss thieves ain't headin' thataway."

"I think we'll be able to pick up their trail on the other side of the river and that's where they'd," nodding to Maggie and Sugar, "catch the trail back to the village. They could make the village 'fore sundown the second day and mebbe we'd get the horses back an' get there 'bout the same time."

"But didn't they take the packhorse?" asked Maggie.

"They got the four new horses and the leopard packhorse. But after tradin' most of the pack of trade goods on one of 'em to the Nez Perce, I think the other packhorse can handle most ever'thing. If not, we can cache the rest and come back for it later. Or, me'n Knuckles could come get it after we get the horses back." He looked to see Knuckles nodding his head in agreement.

Camp was cleared, and horses rigged in short order. As everyone mounted up Sean asked, "Pa, can I go with you an' Knuckles to get the horses back?"

Tate looked at his son's eager expression and answered, "Son, if we knew how many horse thieves there were and where they were goin', I might be willing to let you go, but, since we don't know and have no idea of what we're headin' into, I'd rather you go with the women and take care of them. They need a man along for protection, you know how it is, don't you?"

Sean looked around, sat a little straighter in his saddle and swelled his chest a bit as he answered, "Sure, Pa, I can do that." He gave a sidelong glance to his little sister and grinned. Sadie scowled back and leaned down to talk to her paint gelding, "C'mon Pretty Boy, we can take care of ourselves." She gigged him forward to move up beside Maggie's buckskin.

KNUCKLES CHOSE a crossing just upstream of the sharp southward bend in the Snake River. The sandbar in the middle made the crossing easy, even with the storm swollen waters. The rain of the night before was more bluster than substance, leaving behind wet grass and deeper stream that drenched the leggings of the riders. As the animals stepped from the sandy shore to the grass, the horses rolled their hides and shook the water from their bellies, prompting the riders to grab at the saddle horns to keep their seats.

Tate and Knuckles dropped to the ground and began casting about looking for sign of the stolen horses crossing. Knuckles waved his hand to get Tate's attention and pointed to the ground at his feet. When Tate came near, Knuckles said, "They come acrost hyar," he turned toward the east and pointed, "looks like they's headed up thataway into that ravine. Prob'ly gonna come out on top in some meadow. I think they's a trail up yonder that runs north an' south, so, no tellin' whar they went. But see here," he pointed to the ground at some tracks, "whoever they was, a couple others joined 'em."

After shading his eyes to look up the ravine, Tate turned away, "Then I think it'd be safe enough to start the women back to the village. Whoever they are, I don't think they'd be wantin' to get too close to a large encampment like that." He walked back to stand beside Maggie's buckskin, "Looks like they took off up into the hills yonder." He placed his hand on the pommel of her saddle. "We're goin' after 'em. From the sign, it doesn't look like too many, maybe only a handful, so if we do it right, we shouldn't have too much trouble." He dropped his eyes and looked towards Knuckles, "Like I said before, I'd feel better if you and the kids were back at the village. There's," he nodded his head toward the shoulder of the hill, "the trail yonder that'll take you back. It'll take a couple days, but you should make it 'fore dark tomorrow. "

Maggie looked down at her man, reached down to cover his hand with hers, "You just be careful and if it's a choice of coming home with the horses or not coming home at all, you forget the horses. Understand?"

He grinned up at her, "Of course! You just get the young'uns back to the village. We'll be along directly." He handed her the lead rope of the dapple-grey packhorse and tugged on her sleeve to make her bend down.

She grabbed the back of his head and kissed him, straightened up, smiled, and said, "I'll be waiting." She touched her heels to the buckskin's ribs and followed Pinaquanah and the youngsters.

———

BAANI STOOD beside the trunk of a gnarled cedar, pushed the branches aside and watched the family of whites below as they separated. He grinned as the women took the trail to the south and away from the men. He stepped back away from the tree, dropped over the edge of the small ravine and swung aboard his bay horse. He reined around and started up the hidden trail to go to the others and tell them their plan was working perfectly.

TATE WATCHED HIS FAMILY DISAPPEAR AROUND THE TIMBERED shoulder that held the trail back to the village. Tate kept Lobo at his side, trusting Indy to scout for the women. He muttered a short prayer for their safety, turned back to Shady and stroked the grulla's neck, "Well boy, we've got it to do. Can't let them thievin' renegades or whoever they are get away with them mares. They're the foundation of our new horse herd." With a bit of a hop, he jabbed his foot into the stirrup and swung his leg over the cantle as Shady stepped out after Knuckles.

"If I'ma thinkin' right, they's a purty nice park over the ridge from the headwaters of this hyar creek," drawled Knuckles, pointing his horse to the creek bottom. The tracks of the stolen horses were easily followed as they had been driven into the dry creek bed, taking the easiest way up the wide ravine.

Tate looked at the slopes that dropped into the ravine, "Uh, ya' think we oughta be followin' down here in the creek bed. If I was them I'd be waitin' in the trees to ambush any followers."

"That's what I figgered, an' I'm headin' fer that game trail that sidles along that slope yonder." Knuckles pointed with the muzzle of his rifle to the thicker timber on the north slope of the gulch.

The chosen trail ducked in and out of the timber, breaking into wide clearings and parks, but holding near the trees. The intermittent clearings gave the two random glimpses of the creek bottom and the trail of the horses. The passing of the horses churned up the wet sand and gravel and the tracks were easily seen. The hunters were wary and watchful, kicking the horses into a trot whenever possible. They had to cover as much ground as they could, realizing the thieves would be on the run and maybe headed back to their people. But, they couldn't become careless in their haste to retrieve the appaloosas.

Knuckles reined up as he looked below, motioning to Tate toward the creek bottom. "Lookee there, them two creeks come together an' we need to take a closer look at them tracks!" Without waiting for an answer, Knuckles gigged his horse through the scattered trees, making his way to the confluence of the creek beds. Tate was on his heels and the two slid to a stop, dropping from their saddles before the horses came to a standstill. Knuckles walked forward slowly, rifle in hand, but focusing on the tracks. Tate searched the hillsides for any giveaway of an ambush while Knuckles dropped to one knee to more closely examine the tracks.

"Lookee here," he spoke without looking up at Tate. "See hyar, they was a bunch o' horses taken up this draw 'fore the rain an' two fellers from this bunch cut off up thar too!"

Tate looked where Knuckles pointed, then back at the fork in the trail, "An' the rest of 'em went thataway," nodding his head to the north bound fork. He walked a couple of steps up the draw, examining the sign. "Near's I can tell, there ain't too many with 'em. There's five of our horses, but there ain't 'nuff sign for too many of the Indians. What'chu figger, two, three, more?"

Knuckles examined the tracks, bent down to touch the tracks, "Cain't tell for sure, no more'n three an' they ain't movin' fast. It's almost like they figger ain't nobody comin' or if so, they don't care!"

"Ya reckon those two," nodding to the tracks that took the other creek bottom, "might be up to settin' up an ambush?"

Knuckles stood and shook his head, "You're prob'ly right. The only thang Injuns like better'n stealin' hosses, is settin' a trap!"

"Ya think we could trap the trappers?" asked Tate, looking to his mentor. But even as he asked the question, he thought if he was by himself, he wouldn't need to ask any questions, just act. As he considered, he realized they had no choice but to follow the horses. They weren't looking for a fight, just to get the horses back.

"Onliest thang is, they ain't 'nuff of us to trap anything. Nah, we'd best stay on the trail o' them hosses, but just be mighty watchful in the doin' of it. I'm thinkin' these fellers are Crow or mebbe even Blackfoot an ain't none of 'em to be trusted. They's all cagey, they is."

"Yeah, but we got Lobo an' I think he might be our advantage," answered Tate as he stepped aboard Shady and started back up the slope to the trail. Knuckles yielded the lead to the younger man, knowing he was as skilled and even more-so than any other man of the mountains he had known. Tate motioned for Lobo to lead off and the big wolf gladly started at a lope on the trail through the thickening pines.

The creek bottom split again but the tracks took the ravine pointing to the northeast and the two followed, staying higher on the overlooking slope. Within less than a half-mile, another run-off gulley with puddles of last night's rain still in the bottom, cut their trail and pointed to the larger ravine below.

As the two broke from the trees, a wider steep sided ravine opened its maw before them. The game trail they followed had petered out at the edge of the trees and the precipitous edge of the canyon showed itself impassable. Lobo had dropped to his belly to wait for Tate and turned to look back with mouth wide and tongue lolling. Both men stepped down and Tate lifted the telescope from his saddle bags. He sat on a flat rock, used his knees to support his elbows, and scanned the creek bottom. "They stayed in the bottom, the tracks are as clear as if I was standin' over 'em." He offered the scope to Knuckles but was refused.

The older man walked forward, scanning the shoulder of the hill they were on and pointed, "Looks like we can take that bald knob up 'longside the canyon. It's that, or drop into the canyon and that smells like a ambush to me!"

Tate stood and replaced the scope, "Well, since we know they're down there, if we take the high road, we might make better time and catch up to 'em sooner."

Knuckles grinned, chuckled, "Tarnation, why didn't I think o' that? Let's git a move on then, young'un!"

Their choice proved to be a good one and once clear of the timber, they kicked their horses up to lope. Although it was still a climb, the horses seemed to be anxious to stretch their legs. They slowed to a trot as they neared a long hogback ridge and reined up before cresting. Tate dropped to the ground and in a crouch then a crawl, approached the apex of the ridge and peered over to see the backside of the slope and several runoff gullies that fed the larger creek they followed. There was no sign of life, but he looked to the east to the end of the ridge, knowing that would overlook the canyon. He motioned to Knuckles, scooted back from the crest of the ridge and walked to the end to look into the canyon below.

Knuckles ground tied the mounts and joined Tate. Looking down from their promontory, the opening of the canyon spread out as a receptacle of the many run-off creeks that scarred the basin like the claw marks of some storm riding monster. Motion caught their attention and they turned to see horses coming up a notch in the ridge bank onto the far slope. The east face of the long hillside was littered with the carcasses of tall timber that had been felled by a long-ago forest fire that ravaged the entire mountainside. Yet a wide trail cut through the devastated grey with a swath of green that showed the angled trail pointing to the saddle atop the far ridge.

The five horses were still tethered to the picket line cut from their camp. Led by one man, the five appaloosas strung out in a line behind him and they moved at a leisurely pace as they cut back across the face of the littered slope.

Tate and Knuckles looked to one another, backed away from the edge and trotted back to their horses. As they quickly mounted, Knuckles spoke, "So, if there's only one, he might be the bait fer the trap! An' that hillside ain't got much cover!"

"I hear what'chur sayin', but we still gotta go after him, don't we?"

"Yeppir, that we do!"

Once they topped the ridge, they started at a trot toward the wide creek bottom, but Tate reined up and pointed, "You take that high trail just below the slide rock. I'll give you time to get up there an' then I'll follow the tracks up the face of the hill. That way, if there's anybody waitin' beside the trail, you'll have a shot at 'em."

Knuckles looked where Tate was pointing, scanned the mountainside and nodded to his friend, "Sounds good to me. Wait'll I get to them slide rock 'fore you start out."

Tate nodded, motioned Lobo to wait, and stepped down

from Shady. They were protected from view by some scrub oak brush, and he dropped to the ground to wait. With the bald face of the opposite hillside it was easy to follow Knuckles progress and as he neared the brush at the base of the slide, Tate mounted up and with a motion to Lobo, started toward the creek bottom.

———

RED CROW LED the stolen horses up the face of the mountainside, came to the saddle crossing and led the spotted horses into the trees. He slipped from his mount, tied it off to the closest tree branch and threw the picket line over the neck of the nearest horse, the leopard spotted packhorse, slapped it on its rump and watched as he led the others down the long trail and out of sight. He knew the horses would take the easiest path and follow the scent of the other horses, and that would lead them to the wide park with all the tall grass where the rest of their herd was grazing.

Red Crow had two rifles and trotted back to the ridge to await the white men. He dropped down beside a rock pile, searched the valley beyond and spotted one man riding to the upper end of the long timber covered ridge. He waited and watched, and his patience was rewarded with the sight of the second white man coming from the buck brush and going to the ravine. With another glance to the upper slope, he turned his eyes back to search for a good position for his ambush. Leaving one rifle by his rockpile, he moved a little farther up the saddle crossing and found another position in a cluster of stunted pines. He dropped down to one knee, checked his rifle and the cap on the nipple, brought it to full cock to set the triggers, and waited.

The slide rock was no more than a hundred yards from the edge of the saddle crossing where Red Crow waited. He watched as the white man, with his rifle across the withers of the horse, carefully picked his way across the loose stone. The slide rock was flat granite stones, most with patches of green and orange moss, and was always unstable. Although the trail clearly crossed the end point of the slide, dirt and litter marking the trail, any crossing was perilous. Red Crow waited until the white man appeared to be in the middle of the crossing, and he carefully took a bead on the man. He slowly squeezed the thin front trigger and the black powder exploded with a cloud of smoke belching from the muzzle. Crow paused just a moment to see the result of his shot, saw the horse stumble and the man fall. Satisfied, Crow quickly stepped back to trot to his other position by the rocks.

Crow knew the other white man would have seen the smoke from his rifle and would assume he was still there, but his second position was at enough of an angle from his first, that he hoped to get a shot at the second man. He grinned as he thought of his previous shot and the fall of the man and thought now was his chance to prove himself as good and even better than Baani or Peenaquim. He dropped to a crouch, moved to the rocks and his second rifle, and carefully searched the trail for the other man. With no cover but the downed timber, Crow quickly spotted the horse beside a stack of logs. As he watched, the white man tugged at the reins and pulled the horse behind the stack. Crow waited.

The rifle barrel protruded from between the logs and was aimed at Crow's previous position. Crow brought the sights to bear on the logs and the rifle, over 120 yards away, but visible from his promontory. When the white man's rifle bucked, and the report echoed back from the canyon walls, Crow touched off his rifle. The muzzle spat the cloud of smoke and momentarily obscured the vision of the renegade, but he soon saw the rifle had disappeared and a pale blaze of newly marred wood showed where his bullet must have struck.

Red Crow dropped and started reloading, fumbling with the powder horn and the plug. He nervously measured the powder, poured it down the muzzle, capped the horn and grabbed for the possibles bag and a patch and ball. He seated them in the muzzle, slipped his ramrod from the ferrules and drove the ball into the barrel. He lay the rod aside, dug for a cap, fumbled and dropped the first one, grabbed another and eared back the hammer to place it on the nipple. He looked toward the logs, brought the rifle up as he set the triggers and as he seated the butt against his shoulder, he was suddenly knocked to the side when the grey monster struck him and sunk teeth into his neck. Crow screamed and fought against the wolf as the animal shook his head side to side, trying to tear flesh from the neck of the renegade. Crow kicked, shoved and grabbed at the scruffy neck fur as fear filled his eyes and his heart pounded in his chest. He sucked for air, but blood poured down his throat and he choked and coughed up blood as he weakened. With one last desperate kick, he clawed at the attacking beast, and fell to the side as the animal tore at his lifeless body.

Tate, breathless from his run to the rockpile, called to his protector, "Lobo, back!" The wolf was snarling and tearing, but the familiar voice brought him around and with blood dripping from his jowls, his sides heaving with the exertion, he walked to the side of his man and dropped to the ground beside him. Tate bent down to run his fingers through the wolf's fur and spoke softly, "Thanks, Lobo." Tate stood and looked in the direction of the slide rock, saw Knuckles' horse standing, head down, and no other movement. "Let's go see 'bout Knuckles, boy."

A QUICK SURVEY OF THE SADDLE CROSSING SHOWED THE tracks of the horses taking the trail into the timber below the rise. Tate held his rifle ready as he searched the nearby trees for any sign of other Indians, and when Lobo trotted back after his circle search, he was satisfied and started back to where Shady was tethered by the log pile. He quickly mounted, reined the grulla around, and started picking their way through the greyed logs toward the slide rock and Knuckles.

His first glance showed the horse standing, favoring his right fore-leg that seemed to be dangling at an awkward angle. The shoulder of the horse was scraped and bloody and the saddle hung to one side, stirrup dragging. A moan from behind some buck brush caught Tate's attention and he dropped from his saddle, rifle in hand. He stepped around the brush to see Knuckles, struggling to get up. His forehead was scraped and bleeding, his buckskin shirt torn at the shoulder to reveal another red splotch, and his rifle lay at his side, stock broken.

Tate reached to help his friend to his feet, looked him

over and asked, "You alright? I mean you look a little the worse for wear, but . . . "

"I think so," responded Knuckles, feeling himself all over for any wounds he couldn't see. "I think ever'thin' works," but as he took a step he stumbled and grabbed at Tate's offered arm to keep from falling. "That don' feel good," he observed as he tried to put his weight on his right foot. He winced but pushed down and hobbled a couple of steps, "I think I'll be alright." He reached to his forehead and brought back a bloody hand, looked at Tate and asked, "That look bad?"

"Oh, I dunno, might be an improvement, but we might need to bandage it an' your shoulder too."

"Wal, guess I'm lucky to be alive. I was watchin' them loose rocks, an' one o' them whistle pigs let out a squeal, spooked muh horse, an' he sidestepped." Knuckles was remembering and motioned toward the rocks, "an' 'bout that time a bullet spang off'n a rock, the horse stumbled, an' I went head o'er heels into the rocks an' brush!" He shook his head in wonder at the combination of events that took him from the line of fire and saved his life.

Tate chuckled at his friend, "Ain't the first time one o' them marmots spooked a horse, but he sure picked the right time to do it." Tate looked back toward Knuckles' horse and recognized the leg was broken. He turned to see the man scowl, "Hate to see that."

"Well, while you take care of that, that renegade Blackfoot won't be needin' his horse an' it's tied off up there," he nodded toward the crossing.

"How many wuz thar?" grilled Knuckles.

"Just the one. Didn't even see sign of any others. Don't know where those other two got off to," he looked back at his partner, "You gonna be able to take care of that?" He nodded to the horse.

"Yeah, go 'head on an' get that other'n, we can bandage me

up when you get back." He limped toward his horse as Tate mounted up and started to the saddle crossing to retrieve the Blackfoot's tethered horse. Lobo trotted beside him and when they topped the clearing, Lobo looked to the dead Indian and growled, but didn't miss a step as he followed Tate to the tethered mount. The pistol shot echoed across the canyon and Tate knew Knuckles had done the job.

When they returned, leading the dapple-grey gelding, Knuckles looked up from his perch on a flat top boulder and shimmied to the ground to take the lead of the grey from Tate. As he looked the horse over, he turned to Tate, "I'll say this fer them renegades, they sure know horse flesh. Say, you sure they was Blackfeet?"

"I don't know about the rest of 'em, but that dead one up there is, his moccasins were a dead giveaway."

"Dead giveaway? You tryin' to be funny?"

Tate chuckled at Knuckles comment and stepped down to dig into his saddle bags for something to use as a bandage for his friend's wounds. Knuckles busied himself putting his gear on the horse, who was a little skittish with the white man smell and the saddle he wasn't used to, but the man prevailed, and the horse soon stood beside Shady. Tate wasted little effort cleaning and bandaging the wounds, and soon they were back on the trail after the horses.

KNUCKLES STEPPED DOWN to check the tracks of the horses at the top of the trail. The examination was short lived as he stood and proclaimed, "Looks like just the horses, nobody follerin'. That feller," nodding to the dead Indian,"musta slapped 'em on their way. Course, they'd stay on the trail till they found somethin' interestin', like other horses or tall grass or sumpin', but they was movin' purty good when they took outta hyar." As he spoke he climbed back on his horse and started on the trail. Tate just chuckled and followed.

Knuckles had strapped his broken Hawken behind his cantle, stuffed one of the renegade's rifles in the scabbard and held the better of the two, also a Hawken, across his pommel. He had checked and reloaded the rifle and believed it to be as good as his own. He explained to Tate, "It were good 'nuff to put me on the ground, so it'll do me fine."

It was less than two miles down the draw when the trail of the horses bent away from the creek bottom and cut through the trees. Knuckles stopped, looked back to Tate and said, "Young'un, how 'boutchu takin' the lead. Muh head's botherin' me an I ain't seein' too good. Don't wanna lead us into no trap."

Tate gigged Shady past the grey, looked at Knuckles as he passed and asked, "Anything else botherin' ya?"

"Now if that don't beat all. I reckon! You done seen me get pitched into the rocks, and you knowed it weren't no feather mattress I landed on, an' you ask me if anything else hurts! I'll swan it do, I hurt all over! An' if you was a mite more sensitive to yore elders, you'd be more understandin' of muh aches an' pains. I'll shore be glad to get back to muh woman, Smells of Sugar, cuz she knows how to take care of me, she do."

Tate chuckled at the man's ramblings and motioned Lobo to take the lead on the trail. The breaks in the timber started showing a wide clearing ahead and Tate snapped his fingers to stop Lobo. He stepped down, handed the reins to Knuckles and whispered, "I'm gonna check out that park yonder, mebbe walk aroun' a bit to see if I can spot those other two Blackfeet."

Knuckles nodded his head and motioned Tate on as he bent down to put his elbows on his pommel and ease his soreness a little. He watched as man and wolf moved together as one to approach the tree line quietly.

Tate dropped to one knee beside a big spruce with low hanging branches. He pushed one aside slowly, looking between the others to scan the wide meadow before him. He immediately spotted his appaloosas, still tethered to the picket line and close to one another as they had their noses in the tall grass. He guessed about a dozen other horses were scattered about and none showed any signs of alarm or concern. He searched the tree line around the park, looking for any sign of a guard or anyone watching over the herd.

There was no movement or anything like a tethered horse that indicated the presence of a guard. He watched, thinking, putting himself in the place of one that had been left to watch the horses, and searched for a good place for a look-out. But there was nothing that stood out. The park was in a wide basin with a few shallow run-off gullies that fed the larger creek that emptied into the valley below. It was only partially surrounded by trees, with other areas at the upper-end wide open to ridges and mountains beyond.

Then he had an idea and called Lobo to his side. He motioned to the park and the horses, "Go get the horses Lobo, go fetch 'em to me." He waved his hand toward the horses, looked down to see the wolf staring up at him and repeated his words and motion. The wolf looked to the horses and trotted into the wide meadow.

Lobo's head and the ridge of his back showed above the tall grass, but his stance and trot revealed he was neither attacking nor stalking. Several of the Indian ponies spotted the wolf or smelled him, and their heads came up, ears pricked forward and nostrils flaring. The appaloosas had also spotted him but apparently recognized his scent or knew him as the one they had befriended earlier. While the other horses were alarmed and trotted away from the approaching wolf, the spotted horses held their ground. Lobo slowed his approach, going directly to the leopard spotted packhorse that he knew well, and took the end of the picket rope that had fallen to the ground in his mouth and turned to tug on the rope. The packhorse was reluctant at first, but finally took a step and with the insistent tugging, finally started off at a walk behind the wolf.

Tate was watching every move of Lobo and also searching the tree line for any watchers. He knew if there were any guards, they would move to stop the wolf as he led the animals away, but there was no one. Lobo kept up his pace and led the string of horses directly to where Tate waited, dropped the rope from his mouth and sat down, waiting for his due praise. Tate went to the big wolf, bent down and hugged his neck and ruffled the scruff under his neck. "Good boy! But to tell you the truth, I didn't think you'd do it, but you did! Good boy!" Lobo let his tongue fall to the side and seemed to be smiling at his friend, enjoying the praise.

Tate took the picket rope and led the horses back to the waiting Knuckles who sat up and stared as his partner led the string of spotted ponies to him. "Now, how'd you do that? Weren't there any other o' them renegades?"

Tate grinned, reached down to pat Lobo's head and answered, "I just sent Lobo to get 'em an' he did!"

"Just like that? He did what you tol' him?"

"Ummmhummm, just like I told him."

Tate handed the lead up to Knuckles, "But, I'm gonna walk around a little, see if I can see where them others went to or if they even came up this far. I can't figger this whole thing out, it just don't make sense. There's about another dozen horses back there in that basin and nobody anywhere around."

"Mebbe that was the job o' the one you kilt back yonder."

"Mebbe, but it ain't sittin' right." He dropped his head, motioned to Lobo and called back over his shoulder, "I'll make a circle an' be back."

Knuckles slipped from his saddle, tethered his grey, picketed the spotted horses and found himself a grassy patch in the shade of a ponderosa and stretched out. He covered his eyes with his shapeless felt hat and with hands behind his head, tried to relax his bruised and battered body. He knew the horses would alert him of any approaching danger, but he also knew he was stiff and sore and needed some comfort.

When Tate returned, only minutes later, Knuckles was snoring enough to silence the birds and squirrels, but the horses showed no alarm. Tate toed his friend's moccasins and stirred him awake, "C'mon, we need to be goin'."

"What'dchu find?"

"The two that parted from that other'n came up the creek bed yonder. I think it's the same one from down below, but another'n met up with 'em. That one came from over the slope to the east. They spent a little time together, looked like they had 'em a meal, then they all took off back through that cut 'tween them two mountains." He nodded his head to the east and asked, "You know that area?"

Knuckles scrambled to his feet and stepped into his stirrup to mount up, "Let me take a look," and gigged his horse to the edge of the park. When he broke from the trees, he looked to the two draws the led from the park and to the slope on the east. Beyond the slope, two granite peaks showed their heads like a gateway to the beyond. Tate was behind Knuckles as he turned and said, "Yeah, there's a trial to the right of that peak, that's called Wildcat Peak, that follers a crick down to the lake at the base of the Tetons."

Tate looked toward the east at the mountains, and thought about what Knuckles had said, looked back to him and asked, "To the lake?"

"Ummmhummm."

"That means they'll come to the trail where the women are, the one that leads back to the village."

"Ummmhummm." He paused, looking at Tate, seeing the alarm begin to show in his friend's eyes, "Now, don't go gittin' all riled up. We don't know they're goin' there. They just might have a camp or sumpin', 'sides it's way off their usual raidin' territory. That's right twixt the Crow and Shoshoni country and they'd be in a peck o' trouble if they was found out."

"I don't think they're too worried about much of anything. Why else would they leave a prime horse herd behind?" snarled Tate, digging his heels into the ribs of Shady. The lead line of the appaloosa's pulled tight, but Tate just took a wrap around the saddle horn and started off toward the peaks and the trail between them. He lifted his eyes to the sun, which was just past mid-day, and knew he had to push to get where he was needed. He looked back at Knuckles who followed the horses and slapped at their rumps to goad them on, and Tate knew Knuckles was also angered and worried.

CHAPTER TWENTY-FOUR
JOURNEY

THE WELL-USED TRAIL LED BETWEEN TWO BUTTES AND INTO A narrow opening that gave a breathtaking view of the lake that nestled against the foothills of the Tetons. With the cloudless blue sky, warm bright sunshine, and the cool air of the mountains, it was a sight to be remembered. The crystalline blue lake lay smooth and unmoving, reflecting the granite snow-capped crags in a mirror image, framed by the deep green of the pine and spruce that surrounded the water.

"You won't find anything like that in them ol' schools!" declared Sean as he leaned on the pommel of his saddle and motioned with a head nod toward the view.

Sadie looked to her mom and asked, "Don't they have mountains where the schools are?"

Maggie smiled at the innocence of the child and answered, "Wherever you go, there are beautiful sights to see, but not every place has mountains like that."

Sugar, looking at the panorama, spoke softly as she sat beside Maggie, "I could never leave the mountains. They are my home and have been the home of my people forever.

Those mountains hold the spirits of my father and his father before him."

"That is the way Tate feels, even before he came to the mountains, he and his father felt they called to them. They are as much a part of Tate as he is a part of the mountains." Maggie looked at her friend and added, "But it seems it is becoming more and more dangerous. I was never afraid before, but when I was taken by that Crow, I didn't think I'd ever see my family again. And now, and don't tell Tate this, I'm afraid all the time. Not just for me, but for my children as well."

Sugar sat stoically, waiting and listening, feeling for her friend, but not wanting to interfere. She dropped her eyes and waited for Maggie to say more. Sugar knew, as a woman, it was good to unburden your heart and mind and only another woman could understand.

Maggie looked at her friend, "You probably think I'm wrong or something. But I was so terrified when that man had me, I couldn't hardly breathe, and I didn't know if I would live. I can't imagine my daughter going through something like that."

Sean and Sadie had started on the trail, Indy scouting ahead, and the two women were riding side by side as they talked. The women spoke softly, keeping their conversation between them. Maggie and Sugar had spoken before of the time when a renegade Crow had kidnapped Maggie and almost escaped with her before Tate found her and brought her home.

Sugar turned sideways to face her friend, "I have never been taken by another, and I do not know how you felt. But the Great Spirit delivered you to your husband. You have a good man and a fine family, you are very blessed. Wherever you go, there will always be danger. I have never been to your cities, but I have been told there are bad men there also, is this true?"

Maggie grinned at the simple but profound under-standing of her friend and answered, "Yes, that is true."

"Is there any place that you know where there is no danger?" asked Sugar.

Maggie shook her head, "No, I suppose not."

"We women think men do not always remember things like they should, but we are the same. We only want to remember those things that are good and forget the bad. But we must always speak the truth, even to ourselves."

Maggie smiled at her friend, "Thank you Sugar, you're right."

They rode in silence for a while before Sugar spoke again, "I know what it is to be afraid. When I was young, like Sadie, a Blackfoot war party raided our village. They killed many of our men and took many women and girls captive. One of them was my mother. The Blackfeet took them for their wives and slaves and we never saw them again. For a long time, I was afraid. Every night I would curl up in my blan-kets, and crawl under a buffalo robe to hide so no raiders could find me. Sometimes I am still afraid."

Maggie looked at her friend, wanting to reach out and comfort her somehow, but she could not. "See, you live in a big village and you know what it is to be afraid. We live alone, just me and my family, and we don't have a village to defend us. That's why that Crow was able to take me when he did, we were alone in the cabin." She shook her head in anger as she remembered the time not so long ago when she was taken.

The mountain hugging trail wound through the thick timber, in and out of the bright rays of sun that penetrated the thick forest, and the group had traveled far when Sean reined up at the edge of the trees. Before him was a wide alluvial fan that had been pushed for eons from the mountains into the skirt of the lake. It was split by a broad but shallow stream that had coursed its way from the foothills around Wildcat Mountain and beyond. The alluvial sand, silt, and gravel was patterned by grasses, willows and alder. As they surveyed the flat, a small herd of elk, mostly cows and yearling calves, filed back toward the thick timber.

"Should I try to get one, Ma?" asked an eager Sean, hoping for a chance to prove his skill at hunting.

"No, not this time. We have enough meat and no way to pack out a whole elk."

"Well, it's gettin' late, what do you think, Sugar, any special place you wanna camp?" asked Sean, looking to Pinaquanah.

Sugar moved up beside Sean and pointed to the east across the flat, "See that pointed hill? Just this side of those two lakes? There is a good place just below the point of the hill, in the trees."

"I see it. Alright, it won't take us long to get there an' we'll still have plenty of light to make camp." He looked to his sister, "C'mon Sis, you can ride up here beside me across that flat."

Sadie gigged her horse forward, smiling at her big brother. Indy lay on the trail, waiting for the others and at Sean's motion, started across the broad plain. When they came to the stream, Sugar called out for them to wait and Sean reined up near some willows.

As Sugar approached, she said, "We must watch, there are places that are deep and could take you and the horse under."

Sean looked quizzically at the woman, "Under?"

Sugar smiled and said, "I will show you." She stepped down, walked among the willows and rocks, found a long pole that had been washed down with the last rain and walked near the water. She had gone less than thirty yards downstream and waved for Sean to join her. When he came beside her, she said, "Now, see the water there? It is not deep is, it?"

Sean looked where the stream pushed its way down toward the lake and had been divided into several meandering smaller streams. The area pointed out by Sugar appeared to have a sandy bottom under about three inches of water, a streak of black sand wound like a snake atop the sandy bottom and showed nothing that appeared unusual. Sugar smiled as she walked closer, put the end of the pole into the water and pushed with both arms. The pole seemed to slip through the sand and plunge deep into the smooth bottom, and as Sugar took another grip, within seconds, the six-foot pole was almost totally buried with only a few inches sticking up above the water.

Sean stood with his mouth hanging open and his eyes wide as he stared at the immersed pole. He looked back at Sugar and asked, "How'd you do that?"

"It was not me, it was the sand. My husband calls it quicksand. In some places there are big pools of it, even in the bigger rivers. You must always be careful."

"But how can you tell where it is?"

"You cannot always know. Sometimes, the black sand," she pointed to the rivulet of black, "shows, but other times it does not. You must always be careful, try it first, before you cross."

"Wow, thanks Sugar. I could have gotten us in a mess o' trouble." He looked back upstream where his appaloosa, Stardust, stood ground tied. "What about up there? Is it safe?"

"You look and see and if you think it is, try it with a stick like I did. Then you will know."

Sean did as Sugar instructed, determined it to be safe and led the small group across the shallow stream. Once across he looked to Maggie, "Ma, did you know about quicksand?"

"I've heard your father talk about it, but I've never seen it before."

"Wow, just lookin' at that shallow bit of water, you'd never think it was dangerous, but . . ." he shook his head as he thought about what the quicksand could have done. "Ya just never know, do ya?" he mused and trotted his horse up to the side of Sadie.

Sean surrendered the lead to Sugar for her to take them to the camp-site. As they approached the hill with the rocky top, she led them to the south end of two finger ridges and took them through the trees to a hammock-shaped basin that lay obscured between the two ridges. A blowdown of many years prior had provided a stack of big timbers that still showed green branches that drew the water from the big root ball that rose like a dirt wall at the base of one ridge. This spot had been used as a camp before, perhaps many times, and was well situated in the bottom of the basin. Maggie and Sugar made a comfortable encampment and a fine meal; venison steaks broiled over the fire, cornbread biscuits, onions, and yampa.

"I bet Pa's wishin' he was here for this supper," joshed Sean, savoring his feast."Your pa does a pretty good job of cooking over the campfire," defended Maggie.

"Yeah, but, not as good as you!"

"Well, it wasn't just me, Sugar did her part too. But, enough talk. You need to finish up and check on the horses before you get in your blankets."

"I know Ma, I will," he looked to the tethered horses as he spoke. The clearing was well protected, the small fire was near a wide-spreading spruce that would dissipate the smoke and hide the flames from any observers. These were practices that Tate had always emphasized and Maggie and Sean willingly followed. Sean sat his tin plate aside and went to check the horses. He led each one to water at the small spring fed stream, then tethered them near ample graze. As he returned, he spoke to his ma, "They're all set and Indy'll be sleepin' with us. Anything else I need to do?"

Maggie smiled at her big, little boy and said, "No son, you and Sadie can turn in and I'll be along shortly."

"G'night Ma, g'night Sugar," declared the boy as he anxiously turned to his blankets.

Maggie looked to her Sharps leaning against the grey log back from the fire. She lifted her eyes to the dark shadows of the woods, then up to the darkening skies overhead. The first star of the night was winking between two tall spruce, and darkness was settling faster than she liked. But they would only be without the men for one night, and they might even find the horses early and come riding into camp before the night was over, maybe or maybe not. She picked up her Sharps, checked the cap and load, lowered the hammer on the cap and lay the rifle across her lap. She was sitting on the smooth weathered log, looking at the fire when Sugar spoke, "We will be safe. If you want, we can keep a watch. But the black wolf or the horses will know before we do. We should sleep and if we leave early, we will be in the village before this time tomorrow."

"I know, Sugar. You're right, we should sleep, but I'll stay up a while, I'm just not ready."

Sugar nodded her head and went to her blankets. As she covered herself, she looked to the figure on the log, the light of the fire on her face and the shadows of night behind her, and Sugar spoke to the Creator to ask for protection. Maggie still sat near the dwindling fire when Sugar drifted off to sleep.

The shrill screams of the nighthawks came from beyond

the trees and when they quieted, the racket of the cicadas brought a little reassurance of the undisturbed night. When a great horned owl asked his questions of the night, Maggie slipped under the covers, but lay her Sharps beside her. It was going to be a long night for the redhead.

CALEB, OR BLACK BEAR, AND PEENAQUIM SAT THEIR MOUNTS at the edge of the wide basin. They watched the horses that had been the prizes of previous raids, but this herd was less than half the number they had before the attack by the Crow. Both men, sitting silent, were in thought about the raids, the purpose of their band, and what they were planning now. Baani had been the leader and instigator of all that had been done and, by any measure, the entire campaign was a failure. Among most tribes, whenever the leader of a raiding party failed, he would never lead again until he proved himself worthy to be followed. But both men knew the only thing that seemed to drive Baani was his own arrogance and desire for vengeance. Peenaquim, or Seen From Afar, had joined Baani with four of his warriors. Now there were none and he knew that among his people, he would be seen as a failure.

Their thoughts were interrupted when they heard the approach of a horse, knowing that would be Baani. He rode up beside the two and announced, "You made a good plan! The women have taken the low trail and the men have followed the horses. We can go now and take the women!"

"I thought we were waiting for Red Crow," asked Black Bear.

Baani looked at the man, "Red Crow can take the white men by himself! He is a good warrior!"

Peenaquim slowly turned his head to look directly at Baani, "He is one man, they are men of the mountains and dangerous."

"Ha! Crow will take them from cover. He has two rifles and can take one with each!"

"And if he cannot? Who will guard the horses?" asked Peenaquim, motioning to the herd in the basin.

"After we take the women, we can come back for the horses. Then we will have all we need to start our own village!" declared the impatient Baani, scowling at Peenaquim.

Caleb shook his head as the two Blackfeet argued, thinking to himself that he couldn't imagine any woman that would willingly come into the lodge of a man like Baani. But he also knew it was the way of the Indians, to take the women as captives and make them their wives and slaves. But the thought of making anyone a slave didn't sit well with the big black man. He looked at Peenaquim and Baani, waiting for their decision.

Baani swung his horse around and announced, "We go to get the women!" Peenaquim dropped his head and reluctantly moved out after the man, Caleb following, each for his own reasons, but neither in agreement with the man that led them.

As the trail dropped below timberline, the trees were thick, but the warriors moved quietly through the woods following a game trail that showed sign of the recent passing of a bunch of elk. Some of the trees had fresh rubs from the bulls scratching the velvet from their antlers and sparring with the limbs, the ground dug up at the base of the big pines. The descent from the high country was easy going especially after the challenges of the bald and rocky hillsides near the granite topped peaks. The trail hugged the western slope of the mountain and followed the meandering creek in the bottom, but as they neared the confluence with a larger live stream, the path bent to the west to follow the natural contour of the hillside.

The steep shoulder drove the men into the bottom of the gulch and they faced the brilliance of the sun that rested between the craggy peaks of the Tetons. Baani pointed his horse to the edge of the stream and slipped to the ground to allow the animal to drink. Peenaquim and Black Bear stepped down, gave the horses their heads as they seated themselves on the grassy bank.

"So, you know where these women are camped, or do we have to find 'em?" asked Caleb as he looked to the renegade leader.

"The trail they follow is by the bank of the big lake. Only one way for them to go. We will find them." He looked at the lowering sun, calculating the time to the trail and added, "We can find their camp and take them at first light."

"You think they're gonna just stand up and let you take 'em without a fight?" asked Black Bear, looking to Peenaquim for his response.

"Are you afraid of these women?" snarled Baani, scowling at the big black man.

Caleb had taken on the appearance of a warrior, with items taken in raids and traded for from other warriors. He had fringed buckskin leggings, beaded moccasins, a beaded vest over a bone breast plate, and one arm showed a beaded and fringed buckskin band stretched over his massive bicep. Two notched feathers hung from a short scalplock braid behind his left ear. He looked every bit the part of a Blackfoot warrior. He slowly stood and glared at the smaller

Baani, "Ain't never been a man or woman that puts the fear in me, and that includes you!"

The two men stood staring at one another, neither moving. Baani fingered the knife at his waist and Caleb's fist held the big war-club taken in the fight with the Shoshoni. His free hand clenched and unclenched as his muscles rippled in the bright sunlight. Peenaquim stood and walked casually to his horse, turned back to his companions and said, "We do not have time to fight now, we must travel while there is still light." He swung aboard his horse and started for the trail without looking at the standoff.

Baani dropped his eyes, turned to his mount, and followed Peenaquim. Caleb paused for just a moment, breathed deep and with one hop, bellied over the seat of the saddle, swung his leg over the cantle, and followed the others. His rifle was nestled in the fringed sheath under his right leg, but he held the war club over the pommel of his saddle.

With the willow-lined creek to their left and the tree line to their right, the wide bottomed valley made easy traveling. The fast-moving trio had dropped about two thousand feet in elevation and traveled over ten miles since they took to the trail near Wildcat Peak, but it was still ten to fifteen miles to the big lake below the Tetons and the trail where they expected to find the women. The sun had dropped behind the crags and the long shadows of the mountains crossed the water. Their horses' heads hung low and their feet shuffled as they moved. Even the riders were tired when Peenaquim suggested they camp and pick up their search at first light. Although Baani grumbled, he knew the Piegan was right and he reined up at the end of the long valley. The stream they followed dropped into a narrow ravine and the sound of crashing waters and cascades could be heard from below. They made a dry camp, munched on some pemmican and jerky, then eagerly crawled into their blankets for the night.

———

THE MOON WAS WAXING toward full, but the toe of the crescent snagged the nearest dark cloud and the stars watched as the cloud's companions shaded the night sky to a deep indigo. Tate led the way off the bald knob to take the trail into the black timber. The stream below chuckled over the rocks in the bottom of the steep sided ravine. Tate would occasionally catch a glimpse of the cascading waters as the moon peeked from behind its night-cloak. He trailed the appaloosas on the long picket line and Knuckles followed after. At their last stop before nightfall, the whiskery faced old man chuckled about the other horses that were following their little cavalcade. "Horses are funny sometimes, they shore be social kind o' animals. If'n we'da wanted 'em to foller us, they'da run th' other way, sure as shootin'."

"I think you're right about that. There's been too many times I had to chase after horses and all they wanted to do was play hide 'n seek. But with all them followin' and me trailin' these spotted ponies, ain't no way we're gonna sneak up on those renegades."

"You still think they're after the wimmen'?"

"Don'tchu? What else would they be after? The three of 'em ain't gonna attack your village. They ain't that crazy! And what else could be in this direction?"

"I dunno. Less'n there's some wagons or a trader or sumpin'," drawled Knuckles. "But we're gonna hafta stop a while purty soon, I cain't take much more. My hurts is hurtin' and muh bones is complainin'. You keep pushin', I won't be no good to you if 'n we do catch them hoss thieves."

"Sounds like there's another stream up ahead, an' maybe

some grass for the horses. If there is, we'll stop and rest up a mite. But I ain't takin' too long, we need to catch them 'fore they run onto the women."

In just a short while, the narrow ravine opened to the wide valley with the confluence of the stream they followed and a wider creek in the flat bottom. Tate cut across a brushy shoulder and dropped into the green flat that held shadowed willows and alders along the creek bank. The moon shed the darker clouds and cast its soft light on the valley and the horses were quick to take to the creek for water. Tate dropped the picket line, letting the horses have their way and Knuckles stopped beside him.

"This looks like a likely spot to rest up a mite." He twisted in his saddle, spotted a grassy knoll near the tree line and pointed, "I'll be over yonder."

Tate nodded and looked to the horses. The rest of the stolen horses walked into the valley, followed the spotted ponies to the water and tall grass and within moments, the grassy flat was covered with horseflesh. Tate looked them over as good as he could in the moonlight, then reined Shady back toward Knuckles' grassy lounge and dropped down beside his friend. Lobo dropped to his belly beside the men and watched the horses graze.

Tate was antsy and squirmed around to look at Knuckles, "Here's what I'm thinkin'. That trail by the lake," he nodded toward the silhouetted Tetons in the distance, "is at least twelve to fifteen miles. It ain't gonna be easy goin', but if I take one o' them appys and lead Shady, I can make time an' maybe get to the women 'fore them renegades. You stay here, rest up, watch the horses, an' come down when you're ready. Or, if you ain't feelin' too prime, you could stay here an' I'll come back for ya."

Knuckles lifted up to lean on his elbows, winced at the pain in his shoulder, and looked at his friend. "I think you got

the right idee. I think them wimmen can take care o' themselves, but I'd feel better if'n you was with 'em. You go 'head
on now, I'll be alright. But if'n them renegades come back
after these hosses, I ain't gonna fight for 'em."

Tate chuckled, "Good. We can always get more horses,
but, although I hate to admit it, you're one of a kind."

"You bet your sweet bippy I are! Now, go on, git outta
here!" he waved his hand in a dismissive gesture, dropped to
his back and mumbled something to himself. Tate thought he
heard the man say, "One of a kind," but he wasn't sure.

CHAPTER TWENTY-SIX
CONFRONTATION

ALTHOUGH THE EASTERN SKY HAD YET TO SHOW THE FIRST grey hint of light, many of the stars had tucked themselves away and the moon still hung in the west when Baani folded his blankets and put the leather pad and rawhide cinch on his horse. The simple stirrups hung to the side and he turned one to take his foot just as Black Bear spoke, "In a hurry are ya?"

Baani turned to the man, "The moon gives light to find their tracks in the flat by the lake. We go now, we will find them before they start to leave."

The conversation had awakened Peenaquim and the man now stood beside Black Bear. He nodded his head to Baani, "You go, we will join you soon."

The renegade leader nodded his head and stepped aboard his horse and reined around to take to the trail that paralleled the gorge and the cascading stream. Peenaquim looked to Black Bear, "He will not try to take them before we get there. I think he is afraid to move without others near to help him. He is even afraid of the women."

Caleb turned with a wrinkled brow to look at the Piegan,

"Afraid?" and without a reply from Peenaquim, Caleb's eyes moved as he thought back on the other battles and couldn't remember a time when Baani stood by himself. There was always someone near at hand to join him in any fight. He lifted his eyes to Peenaquim, "Come to think of it, I never did see him fight alone."

Within moments, the two men were on the trail following Baani Sanglant and picked their way carefully through the crowding pines. The moonlight did little on the trails and the deep shadows of darkness made for slow going. By the time they reached the wide alluvial fan that spread toward the lake's edge, the rising sun was bending its long lances of gold to paint the tops of the Tetons.

It was a rugged few miles that followed the twisting and winding creek, and the last stretch forced them from the creek bottom to climb a knob that overlooked the wide flat beside the lake. Baani stood beside his horse, scanning the area, searching for any sign of his prey. Caleb stepped down, as did Peenaquim, and walked to the promontory to look over the valley. Their search found nothing, but as they were turning back to their horses, Peenaquim paused, looking to the opposite side of the wide creek to a solitary rock topped hill. He watched, bent side to side and turning his head to see, pointed, "There!"

Baani and Black Bear came to his side, looked where he pointed and saw nothing. Peenaquim said, "There was a thin line of smoke. There, beyond the point of that hill, but it is gone now."

Baani looked to the creek bottom, pointed, "We will cross there, and take the mountain from this side. They will not expect us to come from there."

Peenaquim looked to Caleb and both men nodded to Baani. They mounted and pointed their horses to the descending trail, to cross the creek and duck back into the timber to take the mountain and their anticipated prize.

———

SEAN HAD GATHERED the horses and busied himself saddling each one. The dapple-grey didn't like the pack and reluctantly stood as Sean stretched up to hang the loops of the panniers on the cross-buck.

"Don't forget the coffee pot!" called Maggie, seeing Sean rigging the packs.

"I know, I just figger it's easier to hang the packs an' then load 'em."

Maggie chuckled at the practicality of her son and busied herself with the bedrolls. Sean walked back to the smoldering coals, picked up the coffee pot and sloshed it around, and tossed the dregs on the coals. The steam and smoke rose in a sudden cloud, chasing Sean back from the hissing. "Whoa! Didn't expect that! Thot the fire was already out!"

Maggie smiled, "There's a lesson in that. Don't assume anything!" she watched the puff of smoke rise through the branches, hoping it would dissipate, remembering Tate's caution about fire and smoke showing your location. It was just a thin wisp that escaped the upper branches but was soon dispelled by the cool morning breeze. She thought no more of it but looked around the camp one last time as she walked to her buckskin. Sugar was mounted and waiting, and Sadie sat her horse alongside. Sean strapped down the panniers and parfleche and turned to mount up.

Maggie marveled at the rose tint on the mountain tops of the Tetons, the reflection of the morning sky behind them. Sugar led the column, Sean leading the packhorse and Sadie and Maggie following. As they came from the black timber that marked the hammock between the finger ridges, the trail opened to ride a shoulder with scattered juniper and overlooked the smaller lake just a couple hundred yards to their left. Although they were anxious to get to the village and were already planning the next day, Sugar led at a leisurely pace, enjoying the beauty of the morning.

Maggie twisted around in her saddle to take in the colors of the sunrise off her left shoulder and movement behind her caught her eye. She turned for a better look, spotted three horsemen coming at a lope toward them. She instantly recognized them as Indians and hollered to Sugar, "Run! They're coming after us!"

Sugar turned for a quick look, saw Maggie waving her arms as she put heels to her horse. The buckskin was bumping into the rear end of Sadie's paint, and Sugar lifted her eyes to see the horsemen coming. Sugar slapped leather and headed for a drop off at the edge of a wide draw just before her. Sean's legs came up wide with feet in the stirrups and he slapped them down to get his appaloosa going. The horse leaped forward, bringing the lead rope of the pack-horse taut, but Sean had taken a wrap around the horn with the lead and the dapple-grey stumbled but caught his balance and was matching stride for stride with the spotted horse.

Sugar's horse ran headlong into the gully, sliding down the slope with Sugar leaning so far back she was almost laying on the rump of her mount. Sean copied her, not slowing a bit and plunged over the edge, taking a deep seat behind the pommel with feet deep in the stirrups as he bent his back over the cantle. The dapple-grey packhorse dropped his rear over his sliding back legs to plow matching furrows over the edge. Sadie reined her horse to a stop before gigging the paint pony into the deep gully. Maggie was pulling her Sharps from the scabbard as she leaned back to give her buckskin balance as he lunged over the edge.

Maggie hollered to Sean, "Watch over your sister, don't let anything get to her!"

"Sure Ma!" he answered, grabbing his Hawken from the scabbard as he threw his leg over the cantle to drop to the ground. He ran to Sadie, helped her down and with his hand on her arm, he practically dragged her to a clump of sage that hung from the gully bank. He pushed her down, "Keep down!" He dropped to one knee beside the clump, checked the load in his Hawken, put a new cap on the nipple and brought the hammer to a full cock as he swung the muzzle up to watch the edge of the embankment.

Maggie and Sugar both scampered to the edge of the gully, dropping to their bellies and laying their rifles across their palms, elbows firm on the ground. Maggie saw the three riders spread out, but they were coming at a gallop, laying low on their horses' necks.

"I'll take the one in the middle," declared the redhead, cocking her Sharps.

"Yes!" answered Sugar, drawing a bead on the rider to the right.

Maggie knew she could take a shot to the middle and reload faster than Sugar with her Hawken. Her breech-loading Sharps used the paper cartridges and she could reload and shoot at least five times in a minute, although she had never timed herself, and never before a charging attacker.

Maggie didn't want to shoot a horse, but the man was barely visible with the flying mane of his charging mount. She drew a breath, trying to calm herself, lined the front blade with the buckhorn rear sight and with her finger on the forward trigger, she squeezed, all the while slowly moving her rifle to keep the sights on the running target. The big Sharps bucked, and belched smoke and Maggie instantly dropped the lever to open the breech to reload. She did not wait for the smoke to clear to see if her bullet scored a hit, but hurriedly dug in her possibles pouch for another cartridge and cap. She heard Sugar's Hawken roar and was reassured by the sound. *They don't know who they're after!* she thought.

THE INSTANT BAANI saw the redhead turn and shout, he knew they had been spotted. He hollered to the other two, "She saw us! Spread out!" he waved as he hollered, and the others reined their mounts wide. Peenaquim to his left and Black Bear to his right. He kicked his horse to a gallop as did the others. Each man bent low to the neck of his mount to urge his horse on and dug his heels into the animal's ribs. The lunging lope gave way to the all-out gallop as the horses sensed the race and stretched out, noses into the wind and hooves digging deep. The junipers whipped past and horses leaped sage and rocks without missing a step. The scattered trees were sparse and the wide bald flat beckoned their fastest pace.

They watched as the four riders and five horses dropped from sight over the edge of the gulley, but they did not slow their pace. The edge was two hundred yards away and they were covering the distance quickly. Before they expected it, smoke blossomed from the line at the draw and the report of rifles ratcheted across the flat. Suddenly, the long-legged bay rode by Baani dropped to his chin and tumbled end over end, sending the renegade leader flying over his head. Peenaquim saw the horse fall, looked back to the gulley's edge, and was suddenly burned across his shoulder and back. The shock of the bullet forced the man to the side, almost unseating him, but he managed to rein his mount into the trees and out of sight of those in the gulley.

Caleb, upon seeing Baani thrown, also reined his mount

away and into the trees. The sudden volley from the gulley had shocked them all and split their force. Caleb reined up, looked to the spot where Baani fell and saw him rise, shake himself, and take off at a run toward the gulley. Caleb kicked his horse into a run toward the end of the draw, thinking he needed to get to the women before Baani, but could he?

CHAPTER TWENTY-SEVEN
FIGHT

TATE STARTED HIS PURSUIT ATOP THE APPALOOSA, LEADING Shady. The sun was shooting arrows of gold past the pink clouds when he came to the narrow canyon and the cascading water. The roar of the falls was muffled by the thick pines as Tate followed the deep tracks of the renegades. With the soil still moist from the recent rains, there was no mistaking the tracks. The trail twisted through the black timber as the first rays of sunlight tried to force their way through the trees. A sudden sound brought him to a quick stop, and the distant blast of another gunshot bounced off the hillside behind him.

He was frozen in place for just an instant, knowing what he feared was happening. He kicked the appy to as quick a pace as the trail allowed, tree branches slapping at his face as he ducked and swerved through the pines. Any other time, he would savor the rich aroma of the woods and the colors of the sunrise as the many shades of pinks and golds were cast upon the granite peaks. But his heart was beating faster, and he had to force himself to breathe as his stirrups and saddle fenders smacked against the spotted sides of the horse. He touched the butt of his Dragoon, felt for his Bowie, and dropped his hand to the stock of the Sharps, trying to get some reassurance of his preparedness, but fear filled him, and he drove the appaloosa through the timber.

————

MAGGIE FUMBLED WITH HER POUCH, grabbing at a cartridge. She slipped the cartridge into the breech, pulled the lever up and dug for another cap. She glanced up to see if she had scored a hit, saw the downed horse and the rider scrambling to his feet. She was astonished to see him start toward her at a run, waving his arms and screaming, a lance in one hand and a tomahawk in the other. She looked to her pouch, searching for a cap, grabbed one, and reached to put it on the nipple, but dropped it in the dirt. She dug for another, grasped it and carefully put it on the nipple. She put her thumb on the hammer to draw it to a full cock but was suddenly knocked backwards down the bank of the gulley. She lost her grip on the Sharps as she fell, her arms flailing trying to stop her fall and still she tumbled down. She scrambled to get to her feet, but in an instant, the Indian was astraddle of her, screaming and grabbing for her hair. Maggie's eyes were wide in fear and she tried to scream but sound wouldn't come.

The Indian, holding her hair in one hand, snatched a knife from his belt with the other and glared at her as he shouted, "Fire hair! You are mine!" He leaned back his head and screamed his war cry to the sky and looked back at the woman, snarling like a mad wolf. He slowly brought his knife toward her throat, when a rifle roared to his right. He looked to see who shot and saw Black Bear jump from his horse and snatch a rifle from a young man by a clump of sage.

Caleb threw the rifle to the side, looked to see blood

coming from his shoulder, then glared at Baani. He took two long strides toward the crazed renegade, and with a side swing from his massive arm, sent the huge war club spinning towards the man. When it struck the shocked Baani, it knocked him off the redhead, but his hand was tangled in her hair and jerked her to the ground beside him. Before Baani could rise, Caleb stood over him, "You ain't killin' another woman!"

"She is mine! I will do what I want!" snarled the downed leader, as he struggled to his feet.

Caleb stepped back and let him rise, slowly moving his hand to the big knife at his back. Baani charged the big man, knife thrust forward, but Caleb expected the cowardly renegade to do just that and stepped to the side, slapping him with his free hand like an impatient teacher. Baani spun around, dropping into a crouch and holding his knife, edge up, snarling. His eyes flared, and he growled, "You are not a Blackfoot! You are not a Black Bear! I will slit you and pour your guts on the ground, then I will take that woman and do what I want!" He lunged forward, sweeping his blade at the belly of Caleb.

The big man sucked in his gut and felt the tip of Baani's knife barely prick his skin. He twisted to the side, and with his long arm and big hand, he clamped down on the upper arm of the Indian, spinning him around and kicked him in the rump, sending him headlong on his face.

Baani was angered as he knew Caleb was playing with him and jumped up to face the man. He glared and screamed and charged, head down expecting to butt Caleb in the stomach and drive his knife in his side. But Caleb swung a massive fist and caught his attacker broad side of his head and knocked him to the ground. As Baani, now on his stomach, pushed himself up, he shook his head and looked back to see a wide grin paint the face of Caleb, teeth showing his mirth.

MAGGIE HAD BACKPEDALED out of the way of the fighters and crawled to the edge of the arroyo to retrieve her Sharps. She sat down, watching the clash, but reloading her rifle. Once the rifle was ready, she held it at her side, ready to bring it into play, but waited. She had been shocked to see the black man who was dressed like an Indian and to know he was one of the attackers, but when he knocked the screaming Indian from atop her and began to fight him, she was confused. Movement to the side caught her attention. Sugar was walking toward her, but the other Indian was behind her, his arm around her throat and a knife in his hand. They walked slowly down the draw and stopped back from the fighters and stood watching. The Indian holding Sugar was watching the fight and Maggie slowly brought her rifle around to aim in his direction, still holding it across her knees.

BAANI STOOD IN A CROUCH, knife swinging back and forth, both men were bleeding, Baani from the side of his face and an arm, and Caleb from his shoulder where Sean had shot him, and the slight cut across his abdomen from Baani. The renegade leader snarled, tossing his knife back and forth from hand to hand, feinted a charge to Caleb's right and the big man stumbled on a root from the sage.

Baani had dropped his lance and hawk when he knocked Maggie down, favoring his knife to take her scalp, but now he climbed the slope of the ravine's bank to retrieve his preferred weapons. He snatched up the lance, grabbed the hawk and turned, hoping to jump from the bank to attack the big black man with the lance. But he turned just in time to see Black Bear's war club tumbling end over end and whispering the death song with every turn as the big agate stoned head obliterated his face.

Everyone sat silent for just an instant, then Caleb turned toward Peenaquim. "Seen From Afar, you are a good man. I said there would be no more women killed and that means that woman you hold."

The Piegan snarled, "You have killed that coward and you dare to question me?"

"Not a question. I'm tellin' you! I've had enough of this, now back off and you can leave."

Peenaquim curled the edge of his top lip, laughed, "If I cannot have her, no one can!"

He lifted his elbow, readying to draw the knife across the throat of the woman he held, but the bark of the Sharps in Maggie's hand blasted, filling the narrow arroyo with the roar and smoke of the buffalo gun. The .52 caliber bullet tore through Peenaquim's elbow, ricocheting at a slight angle to penetrate his neck and tore the throat from the Piegan. He was dead before he hit the ground. Sugar fell to her knees, holding her throat, but her hands came away without blood and she looked at her friend, forcing a smile as she stood.

Unseen by the others, Sean had retrieved his rifle and returned to Sadie's side. He quickly reloaded the Hawken and now stood, holding the rifle at his side with the muzzle pointed at Caleb. "Alright mister, step back away."

Caleb looked at the youngster, let a grin cross his face, "You already shot me once. Ain't that enough?"

Maggie had hurriedly reloaded her Sharps, looked to Sean, stood and took the few steps from the bank to stand in the bottom of the draw, looking up to Caleb. "So, what do we do with you now?"

"Well, you could bandage me up some if it ain't askin' too much," answered Caleb, grinning.

"How do we know you won't try something?" asked Maggie.

"Ma'am, I just saved your life. Now what would I try? Sides, my momma taught me better."

Maggie looked at Caleb, cocked her head to the side as she thought, feeling that this man meant her no harm and answered, "Alright, sit down, over there. But, Sean's gonna keep his rifle on you anyway!"

"That's fine." He looked to Sean and said, "Just be careful with that thing, you're plumb dangerous."

Sean relaxed and motioned to Sadie to join the women as they dug in the saddle bags for something to bandage the man. The girl walked to their side, Indy beside her. Maggie looked over her shoulder at him and whispered to Sugar, "What do you think? Can we trust him?"

Sugar looked to the big man and nodded, "He is a good man."

CHAPTER TWENTY-EIGHT
RECOVERY

Tate stayed on the track of the renegades, pushing the spotted pony to its limits as the trail twisted through the thick timber. He held his arms before his face to fight off the branches that reached for him with every turn, but the appaloosa was a sure-footed horse that took the twists of the trail with ease, yet he was tiring. Suddenly they were in the open, facing the gravel-bedded stream that came from the canyon. To his right, the alluvial fan spread toward the big lake, but the tracks of the renegades cut toward the timber at the back side of the rocky-topped hill. Tate reined up, searched the hillside and gambled. Another muffled gunshot came louder than before, but it wasn't the big boom of a Sharps, more like the crack of a Hawken.

Taking off at a lope, Shady eagerly following and drawing alongside, he pointed the horses to the end of the pair of ridges that fell from the hilltop. He felt the appy stumble and pulled Shady closer. Without stopping to change the saddle, he reached for Shady's mane, kicked free of the stirrups, and with his Sharps in his hand, he bellied over to the grulla.

Once astraddle of his war horse, he dropped the reins of the appaloosa and dug heels to the eager Shady.

The ancient stream bed was thick with buck brush, and Tate kept Shady on the slight slope between the tangled oak and the junipers to his right. Shady stretched out into a ground-eating gallop, and Tate saw familiar tracks cut across his run but didn't slow. Rounding the scrub oak, he aimed for the slight but long bending knoll that followed the edge of the smaller lake. Within seconds, he saw the fresh tracks that came from the hilltop and pointed along the bald flat knoll. It was obvious the horses that made these tracks were at a run, digging deep into the moist soil. Tate leaned down by Shady's neck, looking at the tracks as they kept up the galloping pace, then he rose to look as far ahead as possible.

Suddenly the tracks separated, Tate quickly reined up, leaning back as Shady dropped his rear and dug in his heels to slide. Tate looked back at the tracks and at those before him. In the distance, he saw the rim of an arroyo and most of the tracks led there, but one set turned wide to the left and another set to the right. Lying before him was the carcass of a horse, but he wasn't close enough to see if there was a man also downed.

He knew he couldn't go charging over the bank; there was no telling what had happened or was happening. The unmistakable roar of a Sharps sounded from below, and he dropped low on the neck of Shady as he slapped the grulla's ribs with his legs. His war horse leaped ahead, his long strides taking them into the cover of the juniper. He crossed the tracks of one of the renegades and followed them warily through the scattered trees. At the upper end of the ravine, he saw the renegade's horse tethered to a tree. Tate slipped from Shady's back, ground tied his war horse and dropping to a crouch, he used every bit of cover offered to follow the renegades' tracks through the brush and trees.

He heard talking, an unfamiliar voice, deep but unusual. Tate inched closer, carefully picking each step among the cluttered dry stream bed. Suddenly he recognized Maggie's voice, then Sean's, and he relaxed just a bit, but kept moving stealthily forward. Lobo was at his side, staying every step taken, waiting for any signal from his master. A scraggly cedar stood between him and the others, and he struggled to see through the pungent smelling branches but was unsuccessful. On the other side of the tree stood Maggie's buckskin and Sugar's paint and Tate stepped closer to peer around the blue-needled cedar and saw the red hair of his woman. She was talking to Sugar, and both appeared to be fine and not distressed. He heard Sugar say, "He is a good man."

Tate smiled and stepped around the rear of the two horses and stood silent for just a moment and quietly asked, "Are you sure?"

Maggie was startled and turned with wide eyes, reaching for the pocket Dragoon in the holster at her hip but instantly recognized the smiling face of Tate and broke into a smile. She ran the few steps to him, threw her arms around his neck and pulled him down to cover his face with her grateful kisses. Lobo dropped to the ground beside the two, content in their presence.

Sugar leaned against the buckskin and laughed at the two, "Uh, we have a wounded man to bandage!" motioning to the big black man seated on the ravine bank.

When Maggie pulled back, Tate gave a quick look down the arroyo, saw the body of Peenaquim sprawled on the gravel bottom, the distorted figure of Baani on the slope of the bank, and a big black man seated on the opposite bank. He looked back to the women, "Looks like you've been a little busy."

Sugar asked, "Where is my man?"

Tate grinned a little, "Oh, he's alright. Maybe a little banged up, but he's back with the horses. It takes a lot to slow that man down."

Sugar smiled in relief then pointed at Caleb, "He saved her," pointing to Maggie, "when he killed that one," pointing to the body on the bank. "She," again pointing to Maggie, "saved me when she killed that one," pointing to the body in the creek bottom. "And he," pointing to Sean waving at his pa with his left hand as he held the cradled Hawken pointed toward Caleb, "is guarding that one," pointing toward Caleb, "until we fix him up."

Tate looked down to Sadie, who was standing with one hand resting on the scruff of Indy and grinning at her Pa and waiting for some attention. "And what about you?"

"Sean shot him," pointing to Caleb, "to protect me," she stated matter of factly, like it was nothing unusual.

"And what were you doing, Mr. Tate, while your family was in danger?" asked Maggie, standing with hands on her hips and her head cocked to the side, trying not to grin.

"Oh, I was just taking a ride in the mountains, enjoyin' the scenery, you know."

Maggie strutted up to him and started beating on his chest with her fists, laughing all the while. She knew her man had done everything except part the waters to get to her and the youngsters and would have been near at hand to rescue them if needed. But the fear still stirred in her heart as she thought about what might have happened. She dropped her forehead to his chest and fought back the sobs of dread and relief.

Tate stepped back, bent to give her another kiss, then turned to Sadie. He picked her up and hugged her tight, as he whispered a prayer of thanksgiving to his Lord. He set her down, turned to walk to Sean and as his son stood, he pulled him close and hugged the boy who was growing tall and would soon be a man. When Tate stepped back, Sean turned his attention to Lobo, hugging the wolf close. Tate turned to Caleb and asked, "So, how did you end up with these renegades?"

Caleb, still seated, had been watching the white man with the wolf, but now dropped his head, then looked up to Tate, "I joined up with 'em right after some white men, buckskinners, attacked and killed my wife."

Tate looked at the man, knowing there was a lot more to his story than that simple explanation, but he didn't want to push for it now. "What's your name?"

The big man chuckled, a low rumble coming from deep in his chest, "That one over there," he pointed to Baani, "hung a name on me, Sik kiáá yo, which means Black Bear. That's what they were callin' me. But muh Momma named me Caleb."

Tate nodded, "Last name?"

"Well, didn't rightly have one. But the man that owned me and gave me my freedom was Mr. Winthrop, so I guess that's the closest thing to a last name I might have."

"Alright, Caleb Winthrop, we're headed to the Shoshoni village 'bout a day's ride from here. That's Pinaquanāh's people. She and her husband, Knuckles, have been together for many years and have a son. My family and I will be going on to our home farther south and in Arapaho country. We've got some horses we have to get, they're with Knuckles now, and we'll be headin' out. Now, what might your plans be?"

Caleb breathed heavily as Sugar worked to bandage his shoulder and stomach. She worked quietly and listened but did not speak. Caleb looked at her and back to Tate, "I don't rightly have any plans. Not since I lost my wife. We were going to explore the mountains, and learn about trapping and hunting and such, but the men that said they'd teach us all about that, were the ones that killed her, and they won't be teaching anybody now. I don't have any people, and I reckon I don't have any plans."

"You done with all this," Tate waved his hand toward the two bodies, "or are you still wanting to be a renegade?"

"Nosuh! I told them I had enough blood on my hands and wouldn't stand for any more. That's why I put a stop to it all. I was just so angry . . . " he dropped his head, shaking it side to side, then looked back to Tate.

"Then give me a hand." Tate turned away and went to the body on the slope, motioned to Caleb to drag the other, and the two men placed the dead renegades side by side under the overhanging edge of the ravine. They climbed to the top and pushed the dirt from the top of the bank down to cover the bodies. They gathered some rocks from the edges of the bottom, put them on top of the mound and walked back to the women.

Maggie and Sugar had gathered the horses and stood waiting as Tate approached. "We can get you set up in a camp, or you can go ahead and try for the village, which would you like?"

Sugar and Maggie looked to one another and Maggie answered, "I think we'll go ahead to the village. Sugar thinks we can make it and we'll feel a little safer too." She forced a smile as she looked to her man.

"I understand." He looked to Sean, who had already mounted, "Son, you've done a good job. I'm proud of you, so keep it up and get 'em safe to the village."

"Sure Pa, we'll be alright. There ain't no more o' them renegades, are there?"

Tate chuckled, "No, I don't think so. Caleb says there were only four of them left and three of 'em have gone under and Caleb says he's changed his ways, cuz he don't want you shootin' at him anymore."

Sean smiled at his pa, looked to Caleb who was also grinning, and sat up straight in his saddle, proud of himself. Sadie slapped his arm and said, "Ain't you big stuff!"

Tate walked to Maggie, put his hands at her waist and pulled her close. He spoke softly, "We won't make it till sometime tomorrow, so you see if you can stay out of trouble, y'hear?"

"That's easier said than done!" answered the mischievous redhead, smiling coyly.

"Well, whatever trouble you got brewin', you wait till I get back, understand?"

"Ummmhummm," she answered and tiptoed to kiss him.

"You probably know where we're goin' to get the horses, at least part way," commented Tate, looking back at Caleb as they climbed the trail beside the cascades. "My friend, Knuckles, is with 'em in the park where that stream down yonder is joined with the one from up by Wildcat Mountain."

"I remember a wide grassy meadow beside this stream where another'n joins it, but don't know the name of any of the mountains," answered Caleb. "All this country is mighty pretty though, ain't never seen the like before."

Tate was listening to the man's language and asked, "You have a way of speakin' that's better'n most. You have some education?"

"When Mr. Winthrop brought me in from the field to work with my momma in and around the house, he taught some of us to read and cipher. He said he wanted his chosen few to be able to 'converse intelligently and clearly and to even share our ideas regarding the farm and home.' But we had to keep it a secret because it was against the law to educate a negro in Missouri."

"And you said he gave you your freedom?"

"He had the papers drawn up, but when he died the overseer tried to keep them from me and my wife. When I took them, we fought, and he fell and hit his head. So, we lit out and here I am."

Tate looked at the man, detecting the sincerity in his eyes and wondered what the future might hold for him. It was shortly after mid-day when they came into the wide bottom of the valley where the horses were lazily grazing. Tate looked to the tree where he left his partner and saw the whiskery face grinning back. Knuckles lifted his hand in a wave as the two men neared. He looked up to Caleb as the two men stepped down, reached down to pet Lobo, then went to his fire and took up the coffee pot and two cups, poured them full, and handed them off.

"Well, aren'tchu gonna say anything?" asked Tate, flabbergasted at the man's silence.

"Humm, wal, b'lieve it or not, I wuz kinda speechless. I mean, I've seen muh share of Blackfeet, but I ain't never seen one that was black all over!"

Both Caleb and Tate choked on their coffee, as they tried to laugh at the confused mountain man. Caleb was the first to respond, "I ain't no Blackfoot! I just traded for these things, so I'd fit in. Ain't no stores around that carry muh size clothes!" he declared, chuckling.

"Knuckles, this is Caleb Winthrop. Formerly known as Black Bear of the Blackfoot tribe."

"Ya don't say? Wuz you wit' them whut stole our horses?"

"Yessuh."

Knuckles turned to Tate, "You're gonna hafta fill me in on the details, but I'se assumin' that since you ain't bawlin', the wimmen an' kids're alright."

Tate nodded, but Knuckles wouldn't be interrupted. "So, what we gonna do? Ya ready to take these lop-eared cayuses down the mountain?"

"We are. That's why I brought us some help. I figger we won't make it all the way today, but we should get into the village tomorrow afternoon."

"Wal, let's get a move on!" declared Knuckles, still limping some but not wanting to show it. He waddled to his tethered horse, called back over his shoulder, "I took them leads off'n them spotted ponies, so we should be able to just drive the whole bunch!"

As the sun dropped behind the western horizon and made silhouettes of the Tetons, the small horse herd was pushed onto a grassy flat just past the scene of the attack. Bordered by the Snake River on the south and west, the thick tree-line along the east, and a rising bluff on the north, it was the ideal place to pasture the animals for the night. The men made their camp on the northwest corner of the meadow and staked out a couple of nearby trees to tether their mounts for the night. Knuckles volunteered to cook, and Caleb rigged a lean-to and gathered the firewood. Tate was sent to bag some meat and he chose his longbow for the task. By the time the camp was ready and the coffee hot, Tate returned with the carcass of a young buck over his shoulder. Tate hung the deer on a pole between two juniper and soon had it skinned and quartered. He dropped the back strap by the fire for Knuckles to slice into steaks and hung the rest high for the night.

The three tired men sat by the fire, sipping the hot java, and watching the moon rise into the starry night. Caleb twisted around on the log, uncomfortable with himself. Earlier, he saw Tate lower his head and say a silent prayer before he ate, and he wondered about the man. He worked up his nerve and asked, "So, Tate, you a prayin' man?"

Tate dropped his eyes from the skies and looked to the

man sitting with long legs stretched to the fire, warming the soles of his moccasins. "Yessir, I find prayer to be a comfort and a guide for my life. You?"

"My momma taught me to pray. We had us a field-hand that doubled as a preacher and we all got together in Winthrop's barn to have church. Like you say, it was a comfortin' thing. But not so much since my wife passed."

"Losin' a wife is a mighty hard thing. I grieved for some time when I lost my first wife. Seems like a long time ago but the memory's still fresh."

Knuckles joined in, "That was that Arapaho girl you met after you'n me came down from Fort Union, weren't it?"

"Yeah, she was a fine woman." His eyes glazed over as he remembered and was quiet for a few moments.

"But you still pray an' such. Weren't you angry with God?" asked Caleb.

"Oh, I felt a lot of emotions, anger, fear, disappointment, grief mostly. I mighta been angry with God for a while, but I knew He didn't do it, He just allowed it."

The white of Caleb's eyes showed bright in the campfire light as he turned to look at Tate, surprised. "I was angry, maybe still am. Why would He allow us to come all this way, then allow them men to do what they done? I just don't understand it, Bea was a good woman, never did nobody no harm!"

Tate noticed how Caleb had allowed his emotions to cause him to lapse into the vernacular of the field-hand. It was a common thing for a man, regardless of his training and education, to devolve into the language of his peers and time. Tate thought a moment, "There are a lot of things that happen that we don't and won't understand. That's what faith is all about. His Word says that 'faith is the substance of things hoped for, the evidence of things not seen.' See Caleb, faith is just believing God. Believing God has our best in His plan." He paused, looked to the flames, back to the big man, "You say your momma taught you to pray, did you and your wife ever pray to receive Christ as your Savior?"

The big eyes flared as he looked up to Tate, who was now standing with his foot on the log, his elbow on his knee, and stirring the fire with a long willow stick.

The words came just above a whisper, "Yassuh, we both done that there in the Massa's house by my momma's bed. She done told us 'bout how we was sinners, and the penalty for sin was Hell forever, but that Christ paid that penalty! She said the book in Romans said we had to confess Jesus, believe in our hearts, and pray and call on the name of the Lord and we'd be saved. We done that, right there, together." Tears were running down his cheeks, leaving shiny trails, the drops catching the firelight and glowing red.

It was as if he had been transported into the past and he spoke as he did before his language was changed by his education, but his emotions were raw and real. His lower lip trembled, and he continued, "But I done some mighty bad things. Don't see how God could forgive me."

"What do you mean?" asked Tate, quietly.

"After my beloved Bea died, I killed all those men!" the anger boiled at the remembrance, then he calmed again to continue. "When I rode with them renegades, I killed some others, both Indian and white men. But when I seen what they done to that white woman, it's like I woke up and climbed outta that well o' darkness." The words came as if from within a vast cavern, resonant and deep, rolling like low thunder.

Tate thought for a moment, looked to the man, saw Knuckles scooting a little closer to listen, and said, "Caleb, do you remember when the Bible tells about Christ on the cross?"

"Ummhumm, shore do."

"Do you remember that Jesus said to the crowd, the very crowd that crucified Him, 'Father, forgive them, for they know not what they do.'?"

Caleb looked up at Tate, brow furrowed, eyes squinting as he remembered, "He did that, didn't He?"

"Ummmhummm. You see Caleb, sin is not the act that we do, it's the fact that we disobey God. When we do wrong, or even when we fail to do right, we disobey God. There is no difference between the sin of the crowd that crucified Him and the sins you and I have committed. One is not more terrible than another, it's that we have disobeyed Him." He paused again, "That's why when the woman that was taken in adultery, which by the way was punishable by stoning, was brought before Him, He looked to the crowd and said, 'Let him that is without sin, cast the first stone.' That kinda hit the holier-than-thou hypocrites and they left without a single one picking up a stone. He compared their *little* sins to her *big* sin to show them all sin is the same. And He told the woman, 'Neither do I condemn thee. Go and sin no more.' So, Caleb, the sins that you're thinkin' about, are they worse than crucifying Jesus? Or worse than adultery or any other sin?"

The big man dropped his head into his hands, sobbing, shoulders heaving, and Tate and Knuckles were quiet and still. A short while later, Caleb wiped his face with the offered bandana from Tate and looked to the man, "So, now what do I do?"

"Just what your momma taught you. Why don't you take a walk and have a little talk with God? I'm sure He'd like to hear from you."

Caleb nodded, stood and turned from the fire to walk into the darkness, the moon, not quite full, showing the way. Knuckles looked up to Tate, "What about me?"

Tate was surprised at the man's question, but slowly

grinned and began again to tell his friend about a loving Savior that had paid the price for his sin and was offering eternal life to even a cantankerous old mountain man like him. Knuckles grinned and followed Tate's lead as they prayed together, and Knuckles accepted that free gift of eternal life, bought and paid for by Jesus. They had said their 'amens' and reached for a fill-up for their coffee cups, just as Caleb returned to the fire, smiling ear to ear.

"I'll take a cup o' that!" he stated as he sat back on the smooth grey log.

Maggie had left Tate a bag of johnnycakes and he shared them with the men as they had more strips of venison back-strap broiled on a willow stick hanging over the campfire. The johnnycakes were warmed on the flat rock near the fire right next to the coffee pot. It was a good meal to start the day and the men busied themselves with eating instead of talking. But the silence didn't last long as Knuckles blurted, "Caleb, whatchu need is another wife!"

The big man looked at the wiry little mountain man and asked, "You got one in your pocket or sumpin'?"

Knuckles laughed, "No, no, not hardly. If'n I did, she shore wouldn't stay there long. But here's what I was thinkin'. Back there in that Shoshoni village, there's some wimmen that'd shine if'n they had a big man like you! And since some o' these hyar hosses are your'n, you could pay a bride price for purt' near any of 'em!"

Tate chuckled at the suggestion of his friend and saw Caleb stare at the man like he was looney. Tate added, "You know, come to think of it, there was a slave on the Lewis and Clark expedition. His name was York, wasn't it? Yeah, that was it. They said that when they went into an Indian village the women would gather 'round York wantin' to touch him and be around him. And that was a Shoshoni village too, wasn't it Knuckles?"

"By Jove you're right. Cuz Sacajawea was a Shoshoni an' she was with 'em too."

Caleb chuckled then broke into a belly laugh as he considered what the men had said. He looked at them, saw they were serious and not just funning him, and asked, "So, just what is a 'bride price?'"

"Why, that's whatever the father of the woman thinks she's worth. A good woman'll cost you, oh, maybe five or six horses," drawled Knuckles, grinning. "But you got that many, what with taking that other Blackfoot's pony, an' his rifle, an' his knife, an' ever'thin' else. Why, Caleb, muh boy, you a rich man in the eyes o' the Shoshoni!"

All three men were chuckling as they thought of what the coming days would bring when they entered the village with this giant of a man attired in Blackfoot gear and looking for a wife. It was going to be interesting at the least, and maybe a little bit of fun.

CHAPTER THIRTY

TREATMENT

THE EARLY START WITH KNUCKLES IN THE LEAD AND TATE AND Caleb bringing up the rear saw the remuda make good time through the timber and into the valley that held the fast running Blackrock Creek. With a short break for the midday feedbag for the men and a graze and water for the horses, they were back on the trail and by early afternoon they spotted the tops of the tipis of the village. Knuckles had been grinning all the way, knowing Sugar and Maggie had probably told the village of the big black man that was coming with their men, and he was anxious to see the response of the people. He was certain very few had ever seen a black man, at least not one the size of Caleb. He dropped his whiskers to his chest as he imagined the reception they would receive.

But Knuckles was disappointed, and Tate and Caleb were surprised when they neared the village. Sean rode out to point them to the upper meadow where the rest of the horse herd grazed, and he told his pa, "They have a nice tipi for us set up on the upper end of the camp. It's a big one with a dark brown flap at the entry. Ma's already there an' Sugar's tipi is right close. See ya!" and he kicked Stardust into a lope back to the camp to rejoin his friends. Tate shook his head and grinned at Caleb, "Ain't he sumpin'? When we're huntin' or out in the woods he's right by my side. But here in the village where there's other young'uns, he won't hardly come around."

Caleb laughed a bit, smiled at Tate and said, "Just be glad you've got a son. I didn't have a pap when I grew up, never knew him."

Before they left camp that morning, Tate had encouraged the others to mark their horses in some way to identify them when they were mixed with the herd. He used a strip of buckskin tied into their mane just behind their ears, Knuckles had some trade ribbon for his and Caleb used some of the fringe from his leggings to tie by the withers of his horses. The men had agreed to divide the renegades' horses equally between Knuckles and Caleb, since Tate had the appaloosas.

It was the custom in most Indian villages for the warriors to keep their war horses or their hunting horses tethered near the tipi, but the mounts of the men had been ridden hard and they chose to leave them with the herd for a time of grazing and recuperating. After leaving their gear by the lodge, the horses were turned out and the men walked back to the village.

"I notice you been favorin' that arm and sweatin' a lot. Did the women get the slug outta that wound?" asked Tate as he walked beside Caleb.

"I think they said they'd look at it after we got here to the village. I looked at it, it's still bleeding, and it's festering."

"Let's see what the women have in mind, I'm thinkin' you're sharin' a lodge with Knuckles and Sugar, but we'll see," answered Tate, looking toward the edge of the village and spotting both Maggie and Sugar watching them approach.

Another woman stood by that Tate had not met and he thought she might be the one the others chose to tend to Caleb. He grinned as they neared, seeing a bit of mischievousness showing in the eyes of his redhead.

Sugar stepped forward and spoke directly to Caleb, "This is Wedá Wáipi, or Bear Woman, or Woman that Stands like a Bear. Her father was the Shaman and she learned from him. She will tend your wound," nodding to his shoulder. Bear Woman stood at least a hand taller than Sugar and as tall or taller than most of the men. Her long hair, shining like the wing of a raven, hung in a single braid over one shoulder and reached to her waist. Her tunic was simple but was beaded at the shoulders with elk's teeth across the front. Fringe hung from the sleeves, and her leggings, also fringed, showed beneath the long tunic that fell below her knees. She was by any measure a beautiful woman, but her expression was stoic, and her eyes moved quickly, taking in everything and missing nothing. She turned to Sugar, "Bring him to my lodge," and turned away to walk toward a tipi that was set off from the others and had a long-legged blood sorrel tethered behind.

She ducked, flipped the entry hide aside, and stepped inside. Sugar pointed Caleb to the entry, motioned for him to enter. The big man ducked low, stepped through the entry and stood to look around the lodge. The lining, attached to the inside of the poles, stretched to chest high and was painted with many designs. Parfleches were stacked toward the back, pouches and dried herbs hung above the stack, buffalo robes covered the floor and Bear Woman motioned to Caleb to be seated on a robe at her feet. Sugar and Maggie stood nearby, ready to assist Bear Woman in her ministrations.

She motioned for Caleb to remove his vest and bone breast plate, and then dropped to her knees beside him to remove the bandages of his wound. As she peeled them back, she wrinkled her nose and leaned back, looked to Sugar, "It has festered. I will need hot water. You," motioning to Maggie, "build the fire and put that knife in the flames." She pointed to a long slender knife that lay with other tools on a buckskin nearby.

Tate and Knuckles remained outside and when Sugar came out for the water, Tate grinning, asked, "Is that the woman you picked out for Caleb?"

Sugar looked at their friend and smiled, "She is a good woman. She has never taken a mate, most are afraid of her. She is a proven and honored warrior as well as a medicine woman. Her father is the Shaman, but she is best at wounds. She would be a good mate for the man."

Tate chuckled as he looked to a grinning Knuckles who said, "I tol' ya'. Anytime a woman sees a man whut ain't hitched, they allus set out to get him a mate. It's the way o' wimmen ever'where!" He laughed as he shook his head. "But I've known her for years, taught her to speak English, she's a good woman!"

Tate looked to his friend, "You taught her English?"

"Don't go lookin' like that! I done taught her real good!" declared Knuckles, chuckling.

Sugar had two basins of water and returned to the tipi. Bear Woman smiled as Sugar set the basins beside her. The Medicine Woman used a piece of cloth to wipe Caleb's face, neck and shoulders with the cool water. Then washed the wound with the hot. She looked to the big man, now prone before her, "I will cut away the dead flesh, then I will get the bullet." While she spoke, she made a tea with some dried inner bark of the willow and lifted his head for him to drink. "What I do will hurt, but it must be done. When the bullet is taken, I must burn the wound for it to heal."

Caleb sipped the tea and looked up at the healer, "You go 'head on. I'm ready."

With practiced moves, she began. With each touch, she looked to Caleb and he appeared unaffected by her work, never wincing, never moving, never making a sound. Even after the repeated probing for the bullet and the removal of the lead ball, his expression never changed. The only indication of any pain or reaction was an occasional hesitation in his breathing. When she brought the heated knife, glowing orange, from the fire and held it over the wound, he just moved his eyes, gave a slight nod, and waited.

There is nothing more repulsive than the stench of burning flesh. When the hot blade touched the open and slowly bleeding wound, it seared and sizzled, sending up a small cloud of steam and smoke. And Caleb didn't react, just held his breath for a moment, then relaxed. Again, and again she worked to cauterize the wound and each time, he did not move. When she was finished, she sat back on her heels and lay the knife aside, looked at the big man before her in wonder and said, "I have never seen any man so strong and brave." A slow smile crossed her face as she turned to a nearby parfleche to gather the makings of a poultice. She stole glances at the man before her, each time bringing a smile.

She mixed the poultice from the big yellow leaves of the Glacier Lily and the purple flower and mashed leaves of the Bee Balm, and when ready, patted a handful over the wound and covered it with a patch of soft buckskin and wrapped his shoulder with strips of buckskin. Caleb visibly relaxed and lay his head back, resting it on his free hand, and looked to the woman that had tended him. "You are called Bear Woman?"

"Yes, or Woman That Stands Like a Bear. It is because I

stand taller than most women and I am also a warrior for our people."

Caleb smiled, "I was called Sik Kiáá yo, or Black Bear by the Blackfoot. But my name is Caleb. Thank you for what you did," he nodded toward the bandage. He started to rise, and she put her hand on his chest, "You will stay. I will take care of you. Are you hungry?"

Caleb looked at the woman, let a slow smile part his lips and widen his eyes, "Yes, I am hungry. But don't you have a man?"

"I have not chosen a man. I have not found one suitable." She also smiled as she put her hands to the ground and began to stand. She looked at the big man with the broad shoulders and massive chest, smiled and turned away to step through the entry.

When she stepped outside, Sugar and Maggie looked to her, and Tate and Knuckles noticed a slight nod pass between the women as they grinned and returned to the work of fixing the meal. Knuckles jabbed his elbow to the ribs of Tate and both of the men chuckled. Knuckles mumbled just loud enough for Tate to hear, "That man's done fer!"

THE MATTER of lodging was settled when Bear Woman chose to keep Caleb in her lodge. As a medicine woman, it was not uncommon for her subjects to stay in her lodge for her convenience, but it was just the second day when Caleb came from the lodge to greet the daylight. He moved well and swung his arms to loosen the muscles and feel the effects of the Bear's nursing and healing poultices.

Knuckles and Tate were at what had become their community cookfire and watched the big man flex his muscles, and Knuckles asked, "She treatin' ya right?"

Caleb was surprised to see the men sitting as if they had

been waiting for him to appear, but he walked to them and grinned, "She's a mighty fine medicine woman, she is."

"Ya know, the people are talkin' 'boutchu and what's gonna be happenin' now that you're healin' up, don'tchu?"

"But . . .but . . .ain't nuthin' been happenin'!" declared a flabbergasted Caleb, looking wide-eyed at the men.

Tate and Knuckles could hold it no longer and the two men busted out laughing and were joined by a giggling Maggie and snickering Sugar.

BEAR WOMAN AND CALEB MADE A STRIKING COUPLE AS THEY walked about the village and the woods. It was obvious to everyone that they were suited for one another and Bear Woman's happiness was evident. She was a prominent and respected member of the band led by Washakie, and many of the old women had wondered if there would ever be a suitable mate for her. There had been a few of the warriors of the band that had considered trying to court her, but she was an intimidating woman. A better warrior than most, skilled with every weapon and a proven hunter, most men were intimidated by her. Usually, men chose women that did not take the warrior path. Even Bear Woman had begun looking to other bands when they gathered together for the Sun Dance in mid-summer, but she had become known among all the bands of the Shoshoni people and she was disappointed then as well.

But Caleb was a mountain of a man whose size threatened anyone that might dare to confront him, and his true nature was hidden under the intimidating figure. Yet, Bear Woman had seen the character of the man when she ministered to his wounds and as they talked by the fire in her lodge. Bear Woman had become fluent in English when she learned from the black robes that visited her village when she was a child, and when Knuckles became a part of their band, she honed her skill in the lodge of Pinaquanah.

As they walked and talked, Bear asked, "You were with the Blackfoot that attacked our warriors?"

Caleb stopped and turned to look at her, "It's like I said, they were all I knew, I had no one else. They said the hunters were enemies and they planned the ambush. When the two charged at me, I had to fight or die!" Caleb's mind was racing as he remembered the time in the woods at the side of Baani. He had been full of anger, but that anger was against white men, yet he was a part of the renegades that fought with the Shoshoni. He remembered well when Baani described them as the Snakes and made the sign of the Shoshoni.

Bear Woman looked at this man that she had come to know as a big but very gentle man. They had talked about his time with the Blackfoot and how it ended, but this was the first she heard about the fight with her people. She knew all the warriors that died and had grieved with their families. She glanced back at Caleb and started walking again. They were on a familiar trail that led from the village to a small lake nestled in a little basin less than a mile from the village. The lake had become a favorite place for them to sit and talk and learn about one another.

As they found their familiar grassy knoll that overlooked the lake, they sat down, and Bear Woman turned to Caleb. "We have talked of you becoming a part of our village and that is good. But this must be told to our chief, Washakie. If others found that you had fought our warriors, and some died, you would be seen as an enemy. Our chief and elders are wise, and I would speak for you, and Big Fist and

Longbow would also, but our council must agree before you can become a part of our village."

Caleb dropped his head, absentmindedly pushing some stones around with his finger as he thought, then he looked up to Bear Woman, "I will do whatever I have to, I'm getting to like it here, especially the company."

The woman, a proven warrior and hunter, medicine woman that was respected by all, found herself speechless and stumbling for a response. She let a smile slowly cross her face and leaned forward to accept the embrace of this man that made her feel like she never thought she would.

CALEB WENT to Knuckles and Tate to try to understand what was going to happen. He had told them about everything that happened when he was with the renegades and the story of the hunting party was no surprise. Knuckles began, "Wal, whatchu hafta unnerstand Caleb, most Indian tribes and languages don't even have a word for a lie. Leastways not like the white man. You just gotta be totally honest an' open with 'em." He looked to Tate and motioned for him to say something.

"From what you said, that was the first time you fought with the Blackfoot, ain't that right?" asked Tate.

"Ummhumm," Caleb shook his head as he remembered, "I was blinded by anger and wanted to kill and even be killed!" he struck his fist to the ground as he gritted his teeth at the thought.

"Wal, here's the way it'll go . . ." began Knuckles and explained to Caleb the way the council meets in the tipi and how they'd be seated and when he would be given a chance to speak. As he continued, Caleb listened, learning more of the ways of the people that he wanted to join and nodded as he listened and understood. It was less than an hour later, when a young warrior came to their fire to tell them they were summoned to the council.

Shoots the Buffalo Running, or Washakie, was the chief of the Kuccuntikka or Eastern Shoshoni, and had the largest lodge in the village. Knuckles led the three through the entry and to take their seat across the fire from the chief and other leaders. To the chief's right was Weahwewa, Wolf Dog, the war chief, and to his right was Rabbit Tail, the Shaman. On the chief's left were two sub-chiefs, Owitze, Twisted Hand, and Po'have, the Horse. Other elders were seated around the semi-circle and in another row behind the chief.

Wedá Wáipi, or Bear Woman, sat to the right of Knuckles, facing the chiefs. Caleb was next to Knuckles and Tate beside Caleb. Washakie ceremoniously lifted the red soapstone pipe to the four directions, the heavens and the earth, drew a long puff and passed the pipe to his war chief.

Once the pipe made the circle, Washakie lowered his eyes to the glowing embers in the fire ring, then lifted them to Knuckles. "Wedá Wáipi has spoken of this man and of his fight with our warriors. She has said Big Fist would speak for him." The statement seemed to hang in the air between them before Knuckles cleared his throat and nervously began.

"Wal, chief, I ain't known him long, but I think he's a good man. Any man that can survive bein' a slave on a white man's farm, is quite a man. But he tol' me 'bout what he been through with the white trappers an' what they done to his wife. Now, if'n that'd been me," he nodded his head and pursed his lips, "I'da done the same thing!" He looked around the circle at many heads nodding agreement and added, "Now, far's that set-to with our huntin' party, wal, I don' know much 'bout that. Caleb there, done talked 'bout that more to Longbow, but," Knuckles put his hand on Caleb's shoulder and looked at the big man, grinned, "I'd hafta believe this feller did what he thought was best." Knuckles looked to the chief and fell silent.

Washakie turned to Tate, "Do you see this man as a man of honor and to be believed?"

"Yes, I do. He has spoken from his heart and told me of his life and I believe he is a good man," answered Tate, wanting to say more but knew he must wait for the chief before adding anything.

The chief looked from one of his leaders to another and receiving no response, turned to face Caleb. "Black Bear, you will tell us of these things," nodding toward Bear Woman and back to him.

The Shoshoni as a people were familiar with the waters and wonders to the north. All had heard the thunder from the belly of the geysers, but none had heard the big black man speak. When Caleb began his voice rumbled through the lodge and the elders and others looked to one another as if they were hearing the thunder of the geysers. Many had wide eyes and expressions of surprise, even alarm, but the gentle spirit of the giant that contrasted with the deep voice caught their attention and held them.

"All my life was as a slave and it was a hard life." He bent forward and drew his buckskin top over his shoulders and turned to show his back to the circle. When they saw the back that was crisscrossed with welts and scars that showed years of whippings and beatings, they mumbled to one another, shaking their heads. Several pointed at the mass of scars that covered his back and spoke in hushed tones. Caleb slipped the tunic back on, faced the chief again and continued. "That was all I knew until the Massa, or chief of the farm, gave me and my wife our freedom. We came to see the mountains and learn to live here, but the men that said they would teach us, killed my wife. In anger I killed them." He shook his head at the remembrance, grinding his teeth and the muscles of his jaw tightened and flexed. "The Blackfoot saw that and came to me to go with them to kill more white men. I was angry and wanted blood and went with the one known as Baani Sanglant, Bloody Outcast. They ambushed the war party from this village and in the fight, I killed some warriors as they tried to kill me. After that fight, I was no longer angry. I am not a Blackfoot, but I had no people and no place to go. When we were told to attack the women, I killed the Blackfoot. I was given the name Black Bear by the renegades, I no longer want that name." Caleb dropped his head and sat quietly, waiting.

The lodge was quiet, and no one moved for a few moments until the chief asked, "Do any of our people want to know more?" and looked around the lodge, giving every one and opportunity to speak.

Bear Woman, because she was a warrior and leader of her people, was allowed to speak where most women, if admitted, would not. "If our leaders decide to allow it, I think our village would be made stronger with a warrior such as this. He has killed but not as an enemy. I speak as a warrior of our people and I believe it would be a good thing if he were to become one of us."

Washakie looked to his leaders again, and with no other response, he waved his hand to dismiss everyone but the leaders. They would confer and decide if there would be a future for Caleb with the Shoshoni.

"So, tell me about this bride price," asked Caleb, looking to Knuckles. The big man had fallen into a sullen mood, anxious for the decision of the council and after pacing around the perimeter of the camp had returned to the fire of his friends trying unsuccessfully to get his mind on other matters. He sat on the weathered log, putting his elbows on his knees and looked to Knuckles for an answer.

"Wal, it's whatever the father of the woman thinks he needs to let her leave his lodge."

"Sounds like the slave markets!" grumbled Caleb, kicking a stub of a log toward the glowing coals of the common cookfire. "It ain't right to sell people!"

Tate saw the disgust on Caleb's face and spoke, "It's not the same. With slavery, the slave is offered at a price or bid for at an auction. With the bride price, you are telling the family how much you value the woman. If the father sees you're willing to sacrifice for her, he believes you will take care of her. But if the price is low, he thinks you don't value her and will not treat her with respect and honor. It's him judging your love for her and you pass that test by showing him you value her."

Caleb looked at Tate, slowly lifted his head and relaxed the stern frown that wrinkled his brow and showed understanding with wide eyes and a slow grin. "Now I understand!" He looked to Knuckles, "How many horses did we share?"

Knuckles squirmed and answered, "They was six apiece."

Caleb dropped his eyes to the ground, thinking and scratching in the dirt, "If I offer all the horses, the extra rifle, and the other things I took from the Blackfoot, you think that'll be enough?"

Knuckles looked to Tate and back to Caleb, chuckling, "Now hold on thar. You cain't go givin' him ever'thing!"

"Why not? You said I had to show I valued her?"

"Yeah, but don't go showin' yore stupidity! Leastways, not right off!"

Caleb looked at Knuckles with his brow lowered over his eyes, questioning. A glance to Tate showed the same doubt.

Tate explained, "There are no secrets in the village. Rabbit Tail knows how many horses you have and if you offer everything, well, he'll know you value Bear Woman, but he won't think much of your smarts. See, you need to keep something for yourself to show you are a man of means, that you have things of value and are to be respected."

"I think I understand. So, what should I offer?"

Tate looked to Knuckles, back to Caleb, "Oh, I'd say, maybe three horses and the extra rifle. What'chu think Knuckles?"

Knuckles leaned his one elbow on a knee, stroked his beard with his free hand, thinking. "Sounds 'bout right. I don't 'member any pappy gettin' a better price than that, not since I been here, anyhow."

Caleb grinned, and relaxed as he sat back on the log,

retreating into his private thoughts as he sat quietly and stared at the fire. He was stirred from his moment of solitude when Knuckles whispered, "Here they come!"

Weahwewa, Wolf Dog, the war chief, Rabbit Tail, the Shaman, and Owitze, Twisted Hand walked to the group that included Caleb. Wolf Dog looked up to the big man, "The council has decided. You will be allowed to stay with our village. You killed Shoshoni warriors that have families that will go hungry, you will hunt and make meat for them to show you are Shoshoni. Your name is given by our chief and you will be called Buffalo Thunder."

Caleb stood still, expressionless, but absorbing what was said and a slow grin split his face. He looked to Knuckles and Tate, saw their smiles and he wanted to jump for joy. Finally, he would have a people, a village to belong to and not as a slave but as a man equal to other men. He looked back to Wolf Dog, "I am honored and happy, is there something I else I need to know or do?"

"No," was the stoic reply and the three men turned and left, leaving the group at the fire relieved and pleased. Knuckles stood, extended his hand, "Welcome to the tribe, muh friend."

Caleb shook his hand enthusiastically and asked, "Would now be too soon to take the bride price to Rabbit Tail?"

Both Tate and Knuckles chuckled at the anxious suitor and both volunteered to help the man. As they walked to the horse herd, Knuckles spoke reassuringly to Caleb and told him how to deliver the price, what to do, and how to respond. Caleb, although already showing his anxiety, continually nodded his head and listened to the old mountain man.

The Shoshoni did not hold to special ceremony regarding marriage. While each band of natives had different customs, the Shoshoni way was if the father accepted the bride price, he gave the woman to the suitor and the two were considered married. Most often, the bride-to-be still lived in her parents' lodge and when she was given to the man, he just moved into the family lodge until they established their own. But when Rabbit Tail accepted the bride price without any bickering or discussion, and because Bear Woman had her own lodge, she and Buffalo Thunder were considered married. And it was a smiling Bear Woman that didn't resemble a warrior of the people that welcomed her new husband into her lodge and a happy Buffalo Thunder that followed his new bride through the entry-way and dropped the flap behind them.

IT WAS an impressive entourage that left the Shoshoni village by the pink light of dawn. Tate led aboard Shady, with Lobo and Indy on the scout and Tate trailing the two packhorses, the dapple-grey and the leopard appy. Sadie sat astride her little paint and led her choice of the appaloosas. Sean was atop his stallion, Stardust, and led the larger appaloosa with a spotted rump blanket, and Maggie handled her buckskin as she led the two other appaloosas. They had said their good-byes to their friends who stood at the edge of the village watching them start on the trail to the Togwotee Pass and the headwaters of the Wind River.

The Wind River carried its laughing waters down the valley in a twisting course and was the constant companion of the family that traveled ever south, bound for their home in the end of the Wind River Mountains. The late summer travel was pleasant with their trail passing through many patches of quakies, always waving at the passerby, and the whispering pines whose branches bowed at their passing. Mountain sheep watched silently from rocky escarpments high above while marmots whistled a warning to possible prey. But when the challenging bugle of the royalty of the mountains echoed across the deep ravines, Tate reined up and said, "We're gettin' close 'nuff to home, we oughta take us some fresh elk with us, ya reckon?" He grinned at his family knowing they would be eager to be a part of the hunt.

Tate led them to a shoulder of a clearing at the edge of the aspens, stepped down, and walked to the small stream that cascaded down from the rocks above. He bent to one knee, cupped his hand and brought a handful of cold, clear water to his mouth and sucked it all down, smacking his lips in satisfaction. He turned and smiled at his family and said, "Let's make camp an' we'll hunt a bit 'fore it gets dark."

As Tate expected, by the time they were done setting up camp, and had their supper, the sun just passed the edge of the western mountains and the cool shadows of dusk settled over the edge of the Wind River valley. As Maggie and the youngsters readied themselves, Tate stood by a tall ponderosa, overlooking the tree line and the river below. He watched as a wary cow elk tiptoed from the trees, looking up and down the river bank and the grassy slope before her. She moved into the tall grass, eyes on the still deep water at the wide bend of the river. She was followed by other cows, gangly calves, yearling bulls with just a spike of an antler, and when Maggie came to his side, he pointed at the big herd bull that pushed the rest from the trees.

Tate pointed as he softly spoke, "We'll go down thisaway to those tall willows there where the river turns back on itself. We can make it from those trees on the point there and cross through the deep grass to the willows. From there, we'll find us a spot where we can take our shots." He paused and looked at each one, "We only need two, so we'll have to make sure of our shots. Don't wanna go killin' anything we can't take with us." He looked with a grin to his redhead, "How 'bout you takin' Sean and lettin' him do the shooting. I'll take peewee here and maybe she can get her first elk."

"Really Pa?" asked Sadie as she hefted her Hawken to rest it on her hip. She was grinning widely and hopefully as she looked to her Pa. "Sure, girl, I don't see why not."

Maggie and Sean smiled at the little one, both thinking of their first elk and the excitement each one felt. Maggie looked to Tate, "You sure?" thinking about her tenderhearted little girl.

Tate nodded his head and led the way along the edge of the trees, staying out of sight from the small herd. They quickly made their way to the willows and within moments were in position for their shots. Tate had Sadie use a boulder as a rest for her rifle and pointed out a young bull for her target. The girl was a little nervous, but anxious to prove herself, and was on one knee behind the big rock as she took aim. When Tate got a signal from Maggie that Sean was ready, he whispered, "Whenever you're ready, Sadie girl."

She looked back at her pa, lowered her cheek to the stock and lined up her sights. Her finger slowly squeezed the forward trigger and suddenly the Hawken bucked and roared as it belched the cloud of light grey smoke. Almost instantly, Sean's rifle roared an echo. Sadie was pushed back by the expected recoil, but she kept her feet and stood to look for her targeted bull. The spike bull had dropped to his knees, then fell over to the side, dead. Sean's bull had also fallen, and the boy jumped up and shouted, "I got him!" He started to run to the animal but was stopped by Maggie when she told him to wait for his sister.

The rest of the herd had exploded away at the shocking reports of the rifles and could be heard thrashing through the timber in their flight. The four Saints walked to the downed animals as Tate said, "Now, the hard work begins."

When Sadie looked down at the bull, the red blossom of

blood showing behind his front leg, she looked to the head of the animal, saw its wide sightless eyes and the girl turned to her mother, buried her face against her and cried, "I killed it!" It was not a triumphant declaration from a successful hunter, but a compassionate child expressing sorrow at having taken a life.

Sean looked to his pa and back at his sister, started to speak but the stern expression of his ma silenced him. Tate said to Sean, "How 'bout you takin' your ma and sister to camp and bring back the packhorses. I'll get started on the elk while you're gone."

Every hunter knows the emotions that come when they see their first kill. There is the thrill of success, but that is quickly tempered when the animal that had once walked proudly through the woods and was admired in his life, lies dead and unseeing. It is the knowing that life had been taken from a living creature. The natives know and recognize the giving and taking of life as a part of the circle of life and with each hunt, they give thanks to the Creator and the creature alike, each one having given a gift that will sustain the hunter's life.

Sadie had seen death before. Animals and man as well, but she had never been the instrument of death. The tender-hearted child had loved and adopted creatures of the forest, like Buster the bear cub and Indigo, the black wolf. But she was silent as they walked back to camp, holding her mother's hand, pondering what had happened. She had been anxious to prove herself capable to hunt and help the family, but to see the majestic elk lying in the grass because of her was difficult to accept. She wiped the tears that chased one another down her cheeks and looked to her ma, "I don't ever want to kill anything again!"

· · ·

IT WAS their last night on the trail; tomorrow, they would be back at the cabin. The clear night gave no reason for building a lean-to and the family was in their blankets near the fire. Tate had one hand under his head and Maggie lay her head on his chest as both looked at the myriad of stars that sparkled from the black velvet night. The Milky Way arched across the sky and brandished the muted colors in contrast to the brightness of the bold stars of the many constellations. Tate loved the night and picked out the different figures each time he stared into the darkness. He slipped his hand from behind his head and pointed, "There it is! That's our star!" It was the star at the tip of Orion's sword that they claimed as their own. Maggie smiled and said, "It's beautiful tonight."

Tate pulled her close as he replaced his hand behind his head. Maggie whispered, "I think next spring, Sadie needs to go to school."

Tate caught his breath, dreading the idea of even talking about the subject of school. They had spoken several times on the way home, and now with Sadie's hunting experience, Maggie's thoughts had been reinforced. She continued, "Tate, you know the mountains are no place for a young girl. She needs to have an education and to be around people. She is a very smart girl and a sensitive one. She's not cut out for the mountain life. When those renegades attacked, I was terrified and not just for me. All I could think of was what would happen to my children. I am so afraid for her."

Tate looked down at his redhead, the dim light of the fire dancing on her face, "She's too young to go anywhere by herself!" he declared, fearful of what Maggie would say, but she said it.

"By herself? Oh, she won't go anywhere by herself!"

The words felt like a knife piercing his chest. There wasn't a creature in these mountains, four-legged or two, that could put that kind of fear in his mind and heart. Just the thought of being without his beloved filled him with a dread he had never known. He could stand toe to toe with a monstrous grizzly bear with nothing but a Bowie Knife and would fight it to the death, but this was something he could not fight. He knew his beloved redhead was right.

LOOK FOR BUFFALO BATTLE (ROCKY MOUNTAIN SAINT BOOK 10)

The next installment in the Rocky Mountain Saint series is coming soon.

ABOUT THE AUTHOR

Born and raised in Colorado into a family of ranchers and cowboys, B.N. Rundell is the youngest of seven sons. Juggling bull riding, skiing, and high school, graduation was a launching pad for a hitch in the Army Paratroopers. After the army, he finished his college education in Springfield, MO, and together with his wife and growing family, entered the ministry as a Baptist preacher.

Together, B.N. and Dawn raised four girls that are now married and have made them proud grandparents. With many years as a successful pastor and educator, he retired from the ministry and followed in the footsteps of his entrepreneurial father and started a successful insurance agency, which is now in the hands of his trusted nephew. He has also been a successful audiobook narrator and has recorded many books for several award-winning authors. Now finally realizing his life-long dream, B.N. has turned his efforts to writing a variety of books, from children's picture books and young adult adventure books, to the historical fiction and western genres.